THE Price OF Passage

Alex Grayson

CONTENTS

Chapter 1

"To Heine, please!" The woman spoke the words so effortlessly, as if she weren't about to go to the most restricted area. Timothy, the teleportation guard, gaped at the short woman with tiny freckles on her nose. He gasped for air, unsure if he was breathless because of her beauty or because he had to quickly recall what permits and paperwork were needed to cross into the forbidden area.

"What did you say? Where do you want to go?" he stammered as if trying to buy time or hoping she might change her mind or that he misheard. After all, one can't just teleport to Heine. It requires the highest level of authorization.

He felt the other people in line glaring at him as he waited. Everyone was in a hurry. Somewhere. Only he stood in front of the round-shaped metal gate in his uniform, which hung on him as if it weren't his. He was tall and skinny, with long arms sticking out of his sleeves; his feet were huge, and it was a miracle they found the right size for him at the workwear department, having to write twice to the authorities to confirm the size. His white socks showed at the ankles, and the pant legs flapped in the strong wind as if he were wearing a skirt. His head was small, but his vast ears compensated for it, with large green eyes and a long nose, making him look like a weather vane—an apt comparison, as he always turned into the wind with the papers he had to check to keep them from crumbling.

"To Heine, please," the woman said again, extending her papers with her tiny hand. She smiled charmingly, and Tim felt a bead of sweat start to form on his temple. Women didn't usually smile at him like that; they barely looked at him, just hurriedly handed over their papers, some not bothering to greet him. He had to muster all his strength to keep his hand from trembling as he studied the documents.

"Name?" he asked, trying to stay calm.

"Mara," she replied with quiet strength. "Mara Matthews."

To Tim's surprise, she had all the necessary permits, but he found a discrepancy, secretly pleased because it meant he could keep talking to the attractive woman. "I'm sorry, Mara, but something is missing. You have the permits for the northern sector, but you're missing the EPRS number. Did you apply for it?"

The woman pouted in confusion as if she didn't understand. "What number? I don't understand."

"If you want to teleport, you need to enter the data into the system and get an EPRS number, which you must present here. It is an abbreviation for electronic permit pre-registration system. Can be printed or electronic, but your data must be in the system," Tim recited the oft-repeated rules.

"Since when is this required? Is this another new rule that was suddenly introduced?" Mara tried to smile, but her voice betrayed her annoyance.

"Not very long, indeed; it's been like this for two months since the authorities noticed that one permit was being used for multiple trips because they started forging the permits." Tim was amused that the other passengers in line were increasingly rest-less, so he continued. "Ah yes, the good old days when everyone could travel at will, using their bank card for the trip. However, as expected, there were hacks, the system was breached, and people entered prohibited areas. That's why there are gatekeepers now; if it weren't so, I wouldn't have a job..."

"I didn't mean it that way; I didn't want to offend you or question the legitimacy of your job. I think it's perfect that crossings are monitored like this to prevent unauthorized people from jumping wherever they please. I just didn't know about this number..."

"I'm sorry, but you can't pass without it!" Tim said more serious-ly. "Apply for the number and come back!"

Mara's expression didn't change, but her eyes became more intense. "Please, you don't understand. I need to get there now. It's urgent!"

Tim hesitated, surprised by the sudden change in her tone, feeling a pang of sympathy. "I wish I could help, but can't break the rules. I can't let you through if you don't have the number."

Mara leaned in closer, her voice soft and urgent. "There are things in the northern sector that people need to know about. The government is hiding something. Please, I must get through."

To his surprise, the woman grabbed his hand and slipped some-thing paper-like into it unnoticed. Tim looked down and saw that it was money. His resolve wavered, but he forced himself to stay firm. "I'm sorry," he said again, pressing the money back into Mara's hand and her papers. "I can't let you through; it would break the rules."

Mara's shoulders slumped, but she didn't argue further. "I un-derstand," she said quietly, taking back her documents and the money. "Thank you for your time."

As she walked away, the lights in front of the teleporter glowed yellow, and the image of the woman stood out sharply against the background. Tim's heart pounded wildly. Love at first sight? As she disappeared, he calmed down and turned to the next traveler, who had been trying to get his attention for several minutes. He focused on entering the correct codes and felt that something had changed within him. Usually, he despised this behavior; he didn't like being bribed and didn't think it was right. He considered himself too law-abiding, but the woman's image and expression kept coming back to him. He couldn't get her out of his head.

After closing, he went home, and on the way, he looked down at the valley, the walnut grove. He remembered arriving here one year ago to take over as gatekeeper from the bustling city. It was a massive change for him, a city-dweller. The town was in the valley, and you could see its lights at night. The sleepy little village would be even more desolate if it weren't for the teleporter here. A small stream flowed through the village, and there was always such silence that you could only hear the babbling of the stream, the occasional birdsong, or the woodpecker's tapping breaking this uniform tranquility. He listened to all of this now, but when the teleporter was running, it was loud; each crossing's buzzing sound disrupted this peace, and he understood why the locals were grumpy and had protested against the teleporter. That's why it was only operational in specific time slots; otherwise, it was shut down to maintain the village's tranquility as much as possible.

Tim needed to understand why the teleporter here was out-doors. It would be less noisy inside a building, like in the city. But no one knew the answer to this. The villagers had quietly accepted it as a necessary evil because, let's face it, the many people who came here just to teleport and maybe booked a room or spent their money at the only tavern, which also functioned as a store where the locals could sell their goods, somewhat enlivened the monotony of the place. And, of course, boosted the local economy.

If Tim had ever longed for seclusion, a quiet place, he would have imagined something like this for his retirement. However, he was still too young for such quiet tranquility, and no matter how he thought about it, he couldn't understand how being sent here was a step forward for him, as his boss had explained. Judith had told him that he was entrusted with a critical task that only a wonderful and talented young man like him could accomplish. He had been proud of himself until he arrived and saw that there was nothing great here—just a few travelers who wandered in, and it only seemed like there were many because of the two-hour time slot. So, he was very bored.

When Tim arrived, he was convinced that the place was named Walnut Grove because walnut trees were everywhere, and there was a walnut grove in front of the village. But then he saw that these walnut trees were newly planted, about 10-20 years old. So, the origin of the place's name was shrouded in mystery, and when he inquired about it, some said that when the teleporter was built in its initial form, the final working unit was tested here. This could explain why a teleporter stood here in isolation. When they experimented with it, all the plants died, meaning there could have been walnut trees here long ago, but so long ago that no one remembered. The locals preferred to remember something other than Hendrick Walnut, who developed and patented the teleportation system and experimented with it here since he was from this area. So, when Tim suggested that perhaps the place was named after this inventor, they protested and started cursing him, saying what a good-for-nothing he was and how much they had to endure because of the buzzing machine. Of course, Tim knew this was the case because he had looked into it. He also finds out that when the authorities renamed the place in honor of the teleportation inventor, they quickly planted walnut trees so that no one would think of Hendrick and his invention, which only caused them annoyance.

The locals were afraid of the teleporter. The older folks mainly thought it was the work of the devil. If something terrible happened in the village, they quickly crossed themselves and cursed Hendrick's name, shaking their fists toward the teleporter.

Some locals were proud of the invention and that the teleporter was first tested here. Tim shared this pride, although he had never used it. This teleporter was unique because it transported people to distant continents and was unsuitable for local travel. That kind of travel was characteristic of the newer prototypes. And why wasn't this monstrosity permanently shut down? Although old, with original constructions, it operated surprisingly reliably and was connected to teleporters that were no longer connected to the new ones, for example, because those destinations were no longer accessible or only accepted a minimal number of travelers. Only a few such old teleporters remained, which made this one valuable.

Tim walked home indifferently, recalling these peculiar things. His house was a low building consisting of one large room, built of rough logs with windows all around, which made it extremely bright. It was completely different from his small windowless apartment in the city, on the 17th floor of a tall building. It stood alone on the edge of the village but pleasantly close to the forest, near the small stream that flowed through the entire town. A huge walnut tree grew in his yard; what else? And its rustling and the stream's babbling had a calming effect on his nerves—sometimes too calming, as he didn't know what to do with himself. The only thing he didn't like was that he didn't have a key to the house. There was no lock on it; he propped it up with a stake at night to keep anyone uninvited from coming in, and during the day was unlocked, and to enter wouldn't have been a problem for a thief. At first, this worried him, but then he learned that no one locked anything here; somehow, there was no need. Besides, what could they take from him? He had nothing except his spare uniform and a few books he brought.

As part of his daily routine, after getting rid of his uniform and shoes at home, Tim would go over to Noir, the former gatekeeper who had already retired but had yet to return to the city. The village had welcomed him, and he felt much better here. They would have lunch together, which Sara, an aging local housewife who cooked very well, brought them daily. A free daily lunch was included in the gatekeepers' compensation.

"Anything interesting today?" asked Noir when he saw Tim coming in. He was sitting on the bench in front of his house. This was how he always waited for the young man and their lunch.

"Actually, yes," Tim began, sitting next to the old man and slipping his bare feet out of his slippers. "A woman came, trying to bribe me."

"You should just follow the rules, and there will be no trouble," Noir shook his head. "And remember, no exceptions. You didn't accept it, did you?"

"Of course not!"

"Where did she want to go?"

"Heine. The northern sector. And it's strange because she had all the permits, even from the military unit. Just not the number. The simplest thing was missing." Tim leaned comfortably against the house wall and looked up at the hilltop where the circular metal structure of the teleporter stood. In the village, they felt less of the wind's force, but from here, he could see the sign with the opening hours flapping in the wind.

"Well. I don't even remember anyone wanting to go there." The old man started tapping his pipe against the bench, preparing to light it, which was a lengthy process. It began with Tim needing to remove the tobacco and matches from the table. Tim stood up without being asked and entered the room, which was like his, with fewer windows and yellower walls because the old man smoked his pipe inside, too.

Tim wondered whether he should tell the old man what Mara had said about the authorities, but then he decided not to unnecessarily worry him. He quietly pondered whether he would ever see the woman again. Would she return with the number or find another place with a teleporter who would accept the bribe and let her through? He regretted not examining the papers more thoroughly; something must have been off if she hadn't requested the number from the system. Or did she really need to learn about the new rule?

Chapter 2

S ara, the inn's cook, brought them lunch in a basket. She did this partly because she was excellent friends with Noir and partly because she needed the exercise herself, having spent the whole day standing in the kitchen. Arriving with heavy breaths, Tim rushed to help her carry the heavy pots. The lunch wasn't grand, but Tim devoured it as if it were the most delicious meal in the world. Sara ate with them and was always amazed by Tim: "Oh, you child, you eat so much, yet it doesn't show on you! But I love you for it because you eat whatever I bring you; it's a real joy for me!" She even clapped her hands in delight as she watched Tim eat and clean his plate to the last drop.

After lunch, Tim would stroll over to the neighboring property and his garden, leaving the two elders to discuss the world's affairs. While waiting for data from the central office, he busied himself in his garden. This was his other occupation in solitude. He tended a small vegetable garden. However, he had trouble with it because, being close to the forest, wild animals would come and raid his little plants. His corn didn't even have a chance to sprout because the birds picked the seeds out of the soil. In the previous days, he had been reading about scarecrow construction on his computer, gathering materials for building one. He found old clothes in the attic and a standing coat rack. These dusty items were now piled in his yard, waiting for him to start assembling his own scarecrow.

But starting was difficult. Standing before the pile, Tim wondered if it was worth it. Why plant anything here if, once the seedlings sprouted, the deer would eat them? He had thought about this before and now felt even more disheartened. Mara's image appeared before him, smiling at him in a way no one had ever smiled at him before. He could only hope that his mother had smiled at him like that when he was a baby, but Tim didn't remember it as he grew up in an orphanage. Fortunately, he was an intelligent kid, and they educated him, although no one ever adopted him. He learned gardening from one of the caretakers. They would hoe in the small yard of the orphanage; those few hours were his only connection to something resembling a parent-child relationship. The old caretaker patiently explained to him, showing him weeds and vegetables. He carried heavy water buckets. After the old lady died, he was the only one caring for the small garden.

Thus, gardening always filled him with a pleasant warmth, something he remembered as the highlight of his childhood. He had few other memories. He studied to see the pride in his teacher's eyes, and only he knew how much work it took for them to consider him an intelligent kid. He almost always studied, hiding in the closet or the nearby forest to read, just to avoid playing with his peers, who almost always mocked him for his ears or his thin arms, which even a child's hand could encircle easily.

These were old memories he didn't like to recall. When accepted into the gatekeeper program, he was glad to leave the orphanage and get a small room in the city. He only regretted leaving his little garden because he knew the neatly planted tomatoes would dry up, as no one would water them every morning, and tomatoes are susceptible to drought.

After the city, he was delighted to have a large yard where he could garden, and the digging took up much of his time. Initially, he even tried growing tomatoes, but when he woke up one morning to find a rabbit with big brown eyes looking at him from among his beds and all his little red tomatoes gnawed and hanging, he gave up. He didn't like doing things that seemed pointless. Maybe this was his only flaw—he wasn't persistent in anything. He would rather quit than struggle if facing an obstacle, for he feared failure.

Standing before the pile now, he wondered if it would succeed. Was it worth putting in all this work if it didn't scare away the birds?

He went into the house and sat in front of his computer. It was an older model with a screen, a large box-like controller, and a keyboard. You wouldn't see anything like it in the city anymore, where everyone used holographic projectors controlled by eye movements. He had to learn how to use this old machine, practice typing for a long time, and manage to type with just one finger. But he didn't complain; he felt a kind of nostalgia, as they had similar computers in the orphanage, though they weren't allowed to use them, only seeing the caretakers constantly working on them.

After turning it on, a dark, marshy scene appeared on the monitor, with a sprawling tree in the center. The overall atmosphere of the image was gloomy, with a mysterious bluish tint. For some reason, he was captivated by this picture and set it as his background. He liked it because the bright blue sky peeking out from behind the clouds in the top left corner broke the seemingly dark mood. It was as if he saw a metaphor in the image: behind hopelessness, there was a solution, or there was always a way out, a glimmer of hope.

At one point, he had wanted to travel and see the world, which was why the gatekeeping job attracted him. He had not thought he would always stand in one place while the clients traveled. His sense of adventure amounted to nothing, and he couldn't afford to visit any of his favorite places on his small salary. He had yet to realize the job would be so dull and not just about letting travelers through the gate but also involve severe administrative work. Every afternoon, the central office sent over the EPRS numbers for those whose crossing point was his small town, the Walnut Gate. He had to keep track of these, and once the crossing was completed, he had to close the number and scan the permits and papers.

He didn't enjoy this part. He also retrieved data from his own system on who he had allowed to pass and spent his afternoons closing the numbers for those who had already crossed. When he got to Mara's jump, he hesitated. She didn't have a number, but he knew he had to report it if someone tried to cross without a permit. He also knew that reporting it could get her into trouble, possibly leading to a search for her or the discovery that her permits were fake.

But what if everything was indeed in order with her papers, and the only thing missing was the number? There was no need to worry about it. In such cases, protocol required him to provide the traveler's name, so he entered Mara Matthews's name on the appropriate form, with the rejection reason as "missing number." The mandatory fields required a few more details, including the destination, and when he entered "Heine," his screen displayed an hourglass for several minutes as if there was a problem.

The whole procedure took little time, maybe one or two hours. Tim also filled out the statistics, indicating 23 people traveled today, and one was rejected. The downloaded EPRS number was 67, which was unusually high, but this only meant that many people had registered for travel today; when they would jump was up to them.

After finishing his work, he didn't turn off the computer immediately. He checked the news while making himself some dinner. He wondered if he should have included in the report that Mara had tried to bribe him or mentioned what she had said about the government. No, not that. That would have definitely gotten the girl into big trouble.

At night, he had a terrible recurring dream, causing him to wake up constantly and get very little deep sleep. He was trudging through a swampy marsh, knee-deep in water, going somewhere, and suddenly Mara overtook him. She moved effortlessly as if her path was through the muddy water. While Tim's legs were stuck in the muck, the girl walked above the water as if there were a path, smiling at him with that same expression. Tim reached out to her as if asking for help, but the girl smiled and walked past him, disappearing toward the blue sky. This dream, with its dark mood, repeated throughout the night. Sometimes, Tim drowns in the water or stands under it while the girl stands above him, smiling at him but doing nothing.

Still affected by the dream in the morning, he struggled to get up and was half-dazed. He hurried to the teleporter to be there by 9 AM to welcome the travelers. He could barely see straight and, unlike other times when he arrived early to empty the trash bins and tidy up, he was met with a mess. The wind had battered his little booth, and the sign with the opening hours was hanging by one corner. He didn't have time to fix it or pick up the trash from the ground because the first travelers had already appeared at the bottom of the hill. They hurried with their papers in hand, eager to be the first to reach Tim. Always in such a rush, he shook his head. He remembered a time during a festival when some people spent the night up here to ensure they'd be the first to travel. Back then, so many people traveled that he couldn't let the last ones through because the opening hours had ended.

His thoughts were interrupted when a familiar face appeared behind the next person in line. She was beautiful as ever and smiled charmingly at Tim, handing him her papers more confidently this time. She held Tim's gaze so firmly that he started to feel uncomfortable. He took the papers, and his heart skipped a beat as he received them. He wavered momentarily and hoped no one, especially the girl, noticed this.

"Name?" he asked, trying to sound official.

"Mara Matthews," the woman said kindly, a bit urgently.

All the papers were in order, and even the EPRS number was printed there. He turned to the machine and entered the number; it was valid. Yet something still bothered him.

"Mara, when did you request this number? It says it was requested last week. But yesterday, you didn't even know you needed such a number!" He furrowed his brow as he scrutinized the woman, who continued to smile.

"Tim, I told you yesterday that strange things were happening in the northern sector, and I need to go there to find out. People need to know about it!" She leaned closer to Tim as she spoke, and he could smell her perfume. It seemed odd because Mara was dressed like a hiker, with boots and a backpack. Why was she wearing perfume?

"Are you a journalist? What do you mean by saying people need to know?" Tim inquired.

"Yes, I'm an investigative journalist, but I'm more of a freelancer. I don't work for any famous channel," Mara said, pleadingly at the gatekeeper.

"Mara, but you know journalists need a media permit on top of everything else, right?" Tim hated himself for saying this. He hadn't even thought about it; he just decided not to let her through. Because otherwise, she had everything she needed.

"I need to bypass the authorities, Tim. I'm sure I wouldn't get that permit. The authorities are the ones hiding something. Please, let me through! I already have the number, and you said everything else is valid!"

Tim felt sorry for the woman and was about to let her through, thinking she seemed to have all the necessary documents despite his doubts. But then he noticed Noir walking towards him, accompanied by his boss, Judith.

The gatekeeper within him prevailed, and he knew the proper protocol when something suspicious was detected.

"Mara Matthews, I must confiscate and examine your papers to ensure they're not fake. If everything checks out, I'll let you through tomorrow. So I ask you not to hold up the line; come back tomorrow simultaneously, and you can cross."

Mara stared at him with huge, sad eyes, then looked at her papers. "Tim, please, let me through!"

It dawned on Tim that she had called him by his name, which shocked him into silence. When he saw out of the corner of his eye that Noir and Judith were getting close, he snapped back to reality.

"If you know what's good for you, go now! Come back tomorrow!" His voice was forceful, almost commanding, which even surprised him. Mara followed Tim's gaze, and she seemed to understand when she saw the approaching figures. She turned on her heel and vanished into the crowd.

Tim urgently waved the next person forward, stashing the papers away as if nothing had happened. When Judith reached him, he acted as if he had just noticed them.

"One moment, Tim, just a few words," she said, pulling him aside towards Noir. "Was the person who wanted to cross to Heine here again today?"

Tim was surprised but forced himself to remain calm. "No, not yet today..." He had to clear his throat to hide his excitement.

"If she shows up, let us know. Noir and I will be right here on the side."

Tim nodded and returned to his duties, his thoughts filled with concern for the girl. Tim had yet to learn why he had done what he did earlier. Was he now an accomplice? Had anyone noticed he was talking to the woman earlier? He began to understand why this place had its advantages, being an outdoor teleportation point. There were no cameras. No one could review who had been there and when. It struck him as odd that no one had thought to install a camera on a tree or a pole. Or perhaps it was one of those things he couldn't comprehend. Was this place famous for that very reason? No record of who traveled, just the documents. But who verifies that the person in front of him is indeed the owner of those documents?

He had to, but placing such a responsibility on him based on a poorly taken photograph? He wondered if other similar gates had such strange security measures. In the city, one always felt watched by cameras and drones, but here, there was nothing. This peculiar freedom stirred mixed feelings in Tim.

He hurried with the paper checks, feeling flustered, knowing his boss was watching him. It reminded him of being in school. He tried to perform well, paying attention to every detail.

When the initial rush of travelers subsided and only occasional travelers appeared, Noir and Judith came closer.

"It seems you scared the girl away!" Noir joked.

Tim smiled but also felt slightly offended, sensing the mockery. It reminded him of school, where such jokes flew over his head.

"Why is this person so important?" Tim redirected his thoughts.

"Heine, Tim," Judith replied. She usually had an impeccable appearance, but now her hair was pulled back into a ponytail, seemingly in a hurry. Instead of her usual uniform, Judith wore travel clothes with boots. How peculiar, Tim thought, as if she wanted to blend into the crowd. "I'm sure her papers were fake. And I wanted to ask why you didn't confiscate them?"

Tim felt dizzy. "Well, she didn't seem suspicious, just missing the number!" It became clear to him that Judith was there because he had reported the failed crossing yesterday. Were the Heine crossings monitored this closely?

CHAPTER 3

After two hours had passed and no one wanted to cross, Tim began gathering the papers he would need to scan at home. Noir and Judith helped him pack up, and Tim tried to hide Mara's documents so they wouldn't notice. They agreed to have lunch together.

Tim felt uncomfortable and wanted to get rid of the papers as soon as possible and secure them, so he hurried home, promising to return. Judith had arranged with Sara, the cook, that they wouldn't need the gatekeepers' lunch delivered today because they would be dining at the inn. Sara also cooked for the inn's guests.

Upon reaching his small house, Tim quickly flipped through the papers and set Mara's papers aside. He pondered what he intended to do with them. If he officially submitted them, it might be revealed they were fake, and he still wrestled with whether he would be harming the girl or not. He felt deep down that the papers were fraudulent. With trembling hands, he folded them up and hid them in his mattress to ensure no one would accidentally find them. Then, with swift movements, he changed into more comfortable clothes, slipped on his slippers, and headed to the inn.

The village was even more deserted now. All locals were in their homes, enjoying their meals peacefully during lunchtime. The sound of the creek buzzed pleasantly in the background.

Tim felt he was being watched, and this sensation grew stronger as he approached the inn. Out of his eye, he noticed a curtain fluttering in one of the windows. It struck him like a blow to the chest—Mara could still be somewhere around here. Maybe she hadn't left the village. Why would she, when he had told her to try again tomorrow? Could she be staying here? Why hadn't he thought of this earlier?

The small hallway of the inn was dark, and he moved forward uncertainly, groping his way down the long corridor. Opening the door to the dining room, he immediately saw Noir and Judith sitting at a distant table by the window. To his surprise, the dining room was almost complete. Looking around more closely, he recognized some familiar faces, not locals, but other gatekeepers.

Judith greeted him warmly. "We thought you'd never come, Timothy! Imagine Sara making soup today because there are so many of us. I think we're in for a feast!"

"Do I see gatekeepers from the city here?" Tim asked as he made himself comfortable and looked around, still searching for Mara, but she was nowhere to be seen.

Judith and the old man exchanged a glance as if hiding something. Noir had brought his pipe and nervously tapped it on the table's edge. Tim started to laugh. "I'm not going back for tobacco and matches now!"

"I should have told you to bring them!" Noir shook his head. "Anyway, yes, you see correctly. They're here because of the Heine crossing."

Tim broke into a sweat. So, they already knew about the girl trying to bribe him, but he hadn't reported it. Why had he told Noir!

Sara arrived, bringing pre-portioned bowls of soup to a small serving cart. Tim was glad for the distraction, as it drew attention away from him, and he was sure his face was red.

The vegetable soup steamed hotly, and everyone watched as the cook placed the bowls on the tables. When she reached their table, she winked at Tim and whispered, "Let me know if you want more!"

Judith was surprised by the close relationship. "You've made friends here so well, Tim, although I didn't expect you to be so close with the cook!"

Tim didn't need help understanding what his boss meant. They ate their meal mostly in silence, only exchanging a few words, mostly compliments about how well the cook prepared the food and how lucky the people here were compared to the city with its junky, unhealthy food.

After lunch, as people began to leave the other tables, Judith continued her thought as if they had just been discussing Heine. "You know, Tim, strange things are happening in Heine, and it might be better if you knew about them."

Noir nodded frequently and nervously fiddled with his pipe. Tim imagined how much he must have wanted to light it. If they had eaten at home, he would have smoked both before and after lunch.

Judith continued, "There's an invention that everyone is talking about. Rumors are spreading that they've invented a way to cross without gates. With a small device, you can cross wherever you want. The authorities are already taking steps to ensure it doesn't fall into the wrong hands, but those who have heard about it also want to acquire it. That's why Heine crossings are being closely watched everywhere."

Tim leaned in closer. "Do you mean they might patent it, and we'll be out of a job?"

"You've got it right," Noir interjected. "But that's not the biggest problem, at least not for gatekeepers. The real issue is that this will make it impossible to control who goes where and when."

"More precisely, the authorities will have a problem controlling it," Judith corrected. "But there are still many questions. The key point is that the invention must be in the hands of the authorities and not fall into the wrong hands. That's why no one is allowed out of Heine from now on. Entry is restricted too, but if someone has a permit, they can enter, but they will be closely watched."

Tim shifted uncomfortably, not understanding why they were telling him this. He wasn't usually involved in such confidential conversations. Starting to feel mixed feelings. On one hand, he was pleased that his boss was talking to him like an adult, a colleague whose opinion mattered. Not that they were asking for his opinion, but at least he was getting an idea of what the future held for gatekeepers. With a furrowed brow, he could only think about what he would do if he lost his job. "If the authorities have the invention, can they control it, keep an eye on it?" Tim speculated.

"That's part of it, but it's more about money. If the state gets it, they'll profit from it immensely. And that brings me to why I wanted to talk to you, Tim."

Tim gripped his chair, sensing that he would have to answer for not officially reporting the bribe. Why had he told Noir? "I suppose this is about the bribe," he blurted out.

"Yes, Tim, you should have reported it!" Both of them scrutinized him.

"I know, but I didn't want to get her into trouble. I don't know what got into me... but I promise, if she shows up again, I will report it!"

Judith nodded in satisfaction. "Good, Tim. And the other reason we're here. The people you saw here today will be crossing tomorrow. They are members of the Inquisition, a sort of military. They won't have a number; they must cross without a trace, so they can't be tracked. So, when they come to you and hand you their papers, you will let them through and then erase the crossing from the records."

Judith pulled a carefully folded piece of paper from her pocket, unfolded it, and pushed it toward Tim. The paper had names on it, with codes at the end.

"Take these names with you tomorrow. They won't cross all at once; they'll blend into the crowd. So, you let them into Heine, and then in the afternoon, when you're doing administrative tasks, you delete them using the code at the bottom of the paper." Judith pointed to the long sequence of numbers and letters.

"If I understand correctly, I have to let a bunch of travelers into the restricted area?" Tim asked.

"Exactly. But these aren't ordinary travelers; they're going to track down and bring back those who have crossed illegally because of the invention," Judith replied, urgently pushing the paper closer to Tim.

Tim took the paper, folded it, and hesitantly put it in his pocket. "So, I let them through, delete them, and pretend I never heard of them."

"You're smart, Tim. You know your duty. I told Noir you're reliable, and we couldn't have sent a better gatekeeper here!" Judith smiled.

"That's right, I think you'll go far," Noir agreed.

They broke up the meeting, and Judith went to her room while Tim and Noir walked home in the pleasant warmth. Noir was impatient to smoke his pipe, and Tim kept thinking he couldn't tell the old man anything. Even though he thought of Noir as a friend or at least a mentor, he was more loyal to the authorities.

The administrative work was tiring, and Tim couldn't focus. He made several mistakes and had to start over, and Mara came to mind again. Took out the papers. He thought her residence was listed as the inn, but he didn't understand why she wasn't there for lunch. Then he realized everyone would have been curious about her presence if she appeared among the many gatekeepers. It would have been evident that he hadn't let her through, and that's why she was still in the village. The papers still looked authentic, or had the new forgeries gotten that good?

Tim felt a sudden urge to talk to Mara as it started to get dark. He didn't understand his decision and began to doubt as he walked towards the inn. How could it be that no one could be let through according to the rules, yet some were to be let through without a trace? By this logic, the authorities could let anyone through as they pleased. Another feeling swirling within him was fear for Mara. What if they watched her every move tomorrow, and he had to send her away or let her through? Neither seemed like a good solution.

He went straight to the cook working in the inn's kitchen. She was surprised to see the gatekeeper but greeted him warmly. "Tim, dear! Was the lunch good? Do you want something? Some apple pie?"

Tim couldn't stop apologizing, and after eating his second slice of apple pie and listening to the week's menu with all the ingredients and where they were sourced, he finally gathered the courage to say why he had come. "Sara, do you know which room a woman is staying in? Short, with black hair and big brown eyes?"

Sara was momentarily stunned, clasping her hands together. "Tim, I knew that girl was up to something. I thought it was bad, but is she here because of you?" She jumped up, took some walnut liqueur from the cupboard, and poured two small glasses into them. While Tim sipped the strong drink, the cook downed two glasses. "Is she your city girl? You can tell me!" she grinned at him.

Tim was surprised, maybe even blushed, and it felt good that someone finally wasn't mocking him but believed he could have a girlfriend despite his appearance. He looked at Sara gratefully, and his smile was taken as a yes, though he said nothing.

"She's in room six. She wasn't feeling well today, so she asked for her lunch to be brought to her room. Take her some pie," Sara giggled.

Tim stood up, thanked her for her kindness, and headed up the stairs with the plate in his hand. He had no idea what he was doing, and the walnut liqueur had either slightly gone to his head or given him courage? What if he ran into another gatekeeper or Judith? Having no plan, but as he felt the adrenaline rush through his body, he enjoyed the danger, the thrill of getting caught at any moment. He finally felt alive.

In front of room six, he hesitated again and was about to turn back when the door suddenly opened, and Mara stood there with her coat on as if she were about to go somewhere.

"Tim!" the woman exclaimed in surprise. Tim also stood there for a few moments before lifting the plate and showing it as if that was the main reason for his visit. Mara uncertainly stepped aside and motioned for him to come in.

"The cook is worried about you. She said you weren't feeling well," Tim said, handing her the plate.

"That's kind of you to bring it, but you must know that I'm fine," Mara replied, sitting on her bed and poking at the pie with a fork.

Tim stood uncertainly for a moment before sitting on the only chair in the room, in front of the desk, with a shirt draped over the armrest. He carefully picked up the garment and placed it on the desk.

"How do you know my name?" Tim asked, not what he intended to ask, but it worried him the most. Mara stood up and placed the plate on the desk. She took out a note from the pocket of Tim's shirt and pushed it toward Tim.

The paper listed gate names, each with a corresponding name. He found his own: Timothy Emmons, Walnut Grove. Tim swallowed hard and handed the paper back.

"Why do you want to cross?" he asked.

"The authorities are hiding something that the world needs to know. That's why I want to cross," Mara replied hurriedly.

"Yes, you mentioned that. But can you be more specific? Who do you work for? What is this secret?" Tim asked.

Mara studied the gatekeeper curiously. "I can't tell you specifics. But I can double the money to let me through tomorrow if you want. Did you send my papers for verification?"

"It's surprising how informed you are about our processes." Tim stood up and stepped towards the door. "If you try to bribe me again, I won't speak to you anymore. And don't think I don't know everything about why you want to cross!" His hand was already on the doorknob, angered by the bribery. Then he felt Mara's hand on his arm.

"Wait, Tim, I didn't mean to offend you. I want to cross because of the invention. And it's crazy, I know, that I'm still here because you could have reported me anytime. But I saw something in your eyes. When I first saw you, I knew you were different. That you would understand that what the authorities want isn't right."

Mara moved so close to Tim that he could smell her perfume again. She still held his arm, almost caressing it, and Tim suddenly felt scared. He had never been this close to a woman before. Had lost his virginity in a brothel, but it had never felt like this, breathless and overwhelming. It felt as if he hadn't taken a breath for minutes, and as he looked into her eyes, he almost felt dizzy. He looked away and gripped the doorknob tightly.

CHAPTER 4

Tim stood before Mara, his mind a whirlwind of uncertainty. Should he take the leap, as he had often fantasized, and kiss her? But how? A simple lean, a gentle touch of their lips? He tentatively moved closer to Mara, but his actions were so clumsy and uncoordinated that he could see the worry in her eyes.

"Are you okay, Tim?" Mara asked.

Tim closed his eyes and shook his head. "The cook offered me some terrible liqueur; that's probably why. I'm not used to drinking alcohol," he explained, and to end this horribly awkward moment, he decided to make his escape: "I'll let you through tomorrow. Here are your papers." He pulled Mara's papers from his coat. They weren't neatly folded; he hastily stuffed them into his pocket.

Mara accepted the papers in silence, her disbelief palpable. Tim felt the weight of his decision pressing down on him. "But Mara, you must understand," he continued, "agents are scouring Heine for people like you. There won't be a crossing record, but they can check your identity anytime. It's dangerous there now. You should reconsider and go back home."

"Tim, it's kind of you to worry, but I have a plan. The crossing is the hard part. I have friends there already... and thank you for helping!" Mara took Tim's hand and squeezed it. Tim felt how warm and soft her small hand was and made another uncertain move towards her. Then he got angry because he saw concern in her eyes again, so he turned on his heel and left the room without a word. He hurried away, wanting to get as far from the inn as possible.

All the way home, he was upset. How ridiculous he must have seemed, or maybe, at best, Mara didn't notice his intentions. Then he wondered why she was wearing a coat. Could there be others with fake papers? But she was the only one who wanted to go to Heine. What if they're taking a detour? He should have asked many more questions, but why did these doubts only occur to him now? And then there was the cook. What if she tells Noir what he did today? He had to talk to her before lunch. It would be terrible if Noir passed the information on to Judith. There were no cameras, but the surveillance was very effective. Maybe everyone already knew where he had been. After all, he didn't usually go to the inn every day; he should have planned this trip more carefully, like not taking the main road using the inn's side entrance, but all these thoughts came to him now. He hadn't considered the consequences, and now he had to think of an excuse. If Tim could develop a good story for the cook, Mara wouldn't be found out. No one inside the inn had seen him, after all.

The cool evening breeze felt good on his face, which he felt was burning. Why couldn't he be more decisive? He had wasted his last chance because he would let her through tomorrow. He would never see her again and wouldn't know if he had read her signals correctly. Was she kind to him because she wanted to get through the gate? And for that purpose, maybe she would have even returned his kiss? He didn't like this train of thought. Now, he was glad he didn't dare to kiss her. Had Mara returned it, would it have been because she wanted to cross or found him likable? It was too complicated.

Fully dressed, he threw himself onto the bed, wanting to scream.

Sleep came with difficulty to Tim. He tossed and turned, constantly seeing Mara's surprised and concerned expression before him. Eventually, he did fall asleep, but then he found himself in the marshy landscape again, wading knee-deep in the swamp, heading somewhere. In this dream, Mara appeared beside him, but this time, she didn't pass him by; instead, they walked side by side for a while. When Tim stopped and turned toward the girl, they kissed each other so naturally and effortlessly that it felt as if his mind were mocking him. As if it were saying, "See, this is how it's done; it's not complicated at all."

He woke up several times, drank water, and went out into the yard to get some fresh air because he felt like he was suffocating. But the outside noises annoyed him—the deafening chirping of the bugs and the croaking of the frogs—all of it reminded him of the marsh in his dream.

He could hardly wait for morning because he felt he had messed things up badly, all because of a girl he had only known for a few days, a girl who was crossing over to Heine to certain death, and he was even helping her with it. Who knows why. He had to talk to Sara first and foremost. He needed to divert attention from Mara so they wouldn't be linked together.

Finally, morning came, slowly but surely. Tim hurriedly made himself yet another coffee, skipping breakfast, and headed toward the inn, this time taking a detour through the forest, careful not to ruin his uniform. He slipped in through the side door, startling the cook, who was calmly doing her business in the kitchen, preparing breakfast. It was uncertain whether Tim's early visit or his agitated expression surprised her more.

"Sara, I need a favor!" Tim blurted out without waiting for the woman to offer him a seat or express concern. "Could you please not tell anyone that I was here yesterday looking for that girl?"

"Mara?" the cook stammered.

Tim closed his eyes, feeling this was not going well; she even knew her name. "Yes, her. I'm handling something very secret; not even Noir knows about it. Sara, it's essential. Will you do me this favor and not tell anyone?"

The cook sat there in astonishment, then slowly seemed to understand what she had heard. She nodded, her usual calm expression returning. "Oh Tim, you scared me so much and fright-ened me. Why do you have to burst in on people like that? There's already enough weirdness here. Why do you have to act weird, too? With all these strangers around, do you think anyone tells me why they're here? It's no use asking Noir either; he never tells me anything. I see something is going on here; I'm not blind!"

Tim was taken aback, struggling to follow the cook's thought. "Sara, listen, all these people will disappear from here today, the girl too," he deliberately didn't say her name. "I'm just asking you not to tell anyone I was looking for her yesterday. It would get me in terrible trouble."

He looked at the woman pleadingly, and she smiled at him. "Alright, Tim, I know you're a good boy. I won't tell anyone; you can trust me!"

Tim was grateful, then slipped out through the side entrance, heading toward the gate through the forest. He stumbled several times in his hurry, making the journey longer than usual. When Tim reached the foot of the hill, he could already see people gathering. He had just enough time to place the list of names on his small desk to have it handy. He straightened his clothes and hair to look presentable but needed more time to tidy up the scattered trash. From a distance, he could see Judith and Noir approaching.

They stopped a little distance from the gate, pretending to have a casual conversation while scrutinizing the people in line with keen eyes. Tim also noticed other individuals standing idly by the lines, giving the impression that they were inspectors. He had heard of this before, having been part of several inspections in the city. These inspectors would randomly pull travelers out of the line and check their papers.

But now, these individuals just seemed to be standing around, watching. Tim, with clenched teeth, awaited the people holding their papers. If the paper indicated Heine, he checked the list and let them through without a thorough examination, as Judith had instructed. He noticed that these travelers didn't arrive all at once but were interspersed with 2-3 average travelers in between. After half an hour, nearly all of these Heine-bound travelers had crossed.

Tim was slightly angry that such a heavily guarded area now allowed so many people to pass through. But he couldn't do anything about it because it seemed there were exceptions to the strict rules. The word "corruption" came to mind, and it ned at him. This word didn't fit well into his previously loyal worldview. Somehow, he felt a sense of aversion towards it.

While dealing with the papers, he didn't notice a commotion in the line. When everyone turned around, he looked up as well. A traveler was dragged out of the line, supported under the armpits by two others, and pulled away from the gate. Before that, the traveler must have received a few punches to the stomach, judging by the sounds and the hunched posture. Tim had no doubt about what had happened and knew the inspectors' methods. If someone seemed suspicious to them, they would be subjected to torture.

Then suddenly, Mara stood before him. Tim didn't want to drag out the time to avoid suspicion from Judith and the others, but he wanted to exchange a few words with her. The girl was more nervous than necessary, looking at Tim and the people watching them suspiciously. After the usual official questions, Tim added, repeating what he had rushed through the day before, "Please take care of yourself; you'll be in danger there. I'm sorry you didn't change your mind." He then entered the codes, and Mara started towards the gate.

Every fiber of Tim's being protested, and he suddenly realized what he was doing. Then he thought, if others could break the rules, why couldn't he? He pressed the departure button. The loud buzzing started, the blue light swelled in the round teleporter, and Mara stepped through it without looking back. Tim watched her disappear with worry, and then the buzzing began to fade, and the light vanished.

It worked, and no one stopped him. He felt almost triumphant. This was his first act of defiance against the authorities, and he couldn't help but marvel at his courage. He had done it.

And the world went on. More papers, more codes.

Then suddenly, the travelers were all gone, and Noir and Judith approached the gatekeeper.

"Did everyone on the list go through?" Judith asked. Tim nodded and began organizing the documents in the folder for the afternoon's administration. Judith continued, "Could you take care of the ones on the list before lunch?"

Tim also intended to delete Mara from the system as quickly as possible, but Judith didn't need to know that. "Of course, I'll take care of it quickly."

"Come up to the inn for lunch again," Noir called after him. And Tim hurried, afraid that someone might notice Mara's name in the system and download it.

At home, with trembling hands, he took out the papers and started deleting Mara. Since he didn't need to scan any documents, he changed the first letter of her name to S, as if it had been a typo. If they somehow retrieved these records from the system, there would be no trace of Mara. The deleted code was extended to two lines of numbers and letter combinations. Despite his efforts, he messed it up several times and had to start over. It was already lunchtime, and his stomach was growling. By the time he finished with everything, it was past one o'clock.

He took the list with him and hurried to the inn. Sara was the first to look up at him at the door, visibly relieved, and quickly brought him his lunch. "I was so worried that something happened to you, Tim. I know you wouldn't miss a meal!"

They had both finished eating, Judith sat a bit sullenly, and Noir was puffing on his pipe, having remembered to bring his supplies this time, unfazed by the potential annoyance to others.

Tim ate quickly, then handed the paper with the names to Judith.

"Thank you, Tim. I'll stay for a few more days because we found counterfeit papers that we couldn't tell were fake. There might be more inspectors around the gate."

"Does that mean they're checking my work?" Tim asked, frowning.

"Not necessarily your work, but there will be more people helping you spot suspicious things. Due to the limited number of rooms at the inn, some people might be lodged with you and Noir."

Tim nodded, but his mind was more occupied with the circumstances that might reveal what he had done today. Not from the system. Again, it was Sara he worried about. Could he really trust her?

CHAPTER 5

Tim's uncertainty made him anxious. Since he started working as a gatekeeper, it was the first time he wasn't bored. The silence of his apartment, which had once been a refuge, now felt like a prison. Guilt consumed him, constantly thinking about what he had done and how he would react or explain himself if it was discovered. He couldn't shake the fear of the impending consequences – disciplinary action, torture, or even worse, suspension or immediate imprisonment. But the doubts about the system he had so loyally served were more profound than the fear.

Tim found himself trapped in a relentless battle within his mind, pacing back and forth in his cramped living room. The memory of the moment he had allowed Mara to pass through the gate haunted him. He could still see the sincerity in her eyes and hear the conviction in her voice. He believed her, but this belief came at a steep price. He was torn between his duty to uphold the law and his growing conviction about the system's inherent flaws.

Hours passed, but the minutes crawled so slowly that Tim sometimes wished someone would catch him so he wouldn't have to think anymore. He wanted to go to Noir but couldn't face him and pretend everything was fine. Yet Tim couldn't stay in the solitude of his room either, so he went outside to the yard, passing by the clutter he had brought down from the attic to make a scarecrow. He had resolved to occupy himself to distract his mind, but he only managed to lift the worn-out clothes stand. Instead, he took long walks around the town, hoping the fresh air would clear his head. But wherever he went, he encountered reminders of his mistake – the grim faces of strangers and even the locals seemed sullen, and the now silent, ominous teleport gate looming towards the village.

As the evening shadows lengthened, Tim knew he had to return home. The administration, the closure of numbers, still awaited him. He wandered aimlessly through the village, his senses on high alert. Suddenly, a figure with a hood pulled low over his eyes joined him in a quiet little street, their presence sending a shiver down Tim's spine.

"I need to talk to you about Mara. Come to the walnut grove, but make sure no one sees you following," said the strange figure, who then quickened his pace and headed towards the grove.

Tim's heart pounded. He knew it could be a trap, but something told him he had to meet him. He needed to know more about what Mara was trying to achieve and wanted answers.

He took a detour towards the grove, stepping cautiously and constantly looking over his shoulder to see if he was being followed. As he entered the dense shadows of the trees and because it was getting dark, he barely noticed the figure he was supposed to meet.

"Tim," whispered a voice from the shadows. He turned around and saw the hooded figure stepping forward cautiously and covertly.

"Who are you?" Tim asked, trying to keep his voice steady.

The figure pulled back his hood, revealing a slightly stubbled face. "My name is Peter. I'm a friend of Mara's."

Tim's tension eased slightly. "What do you want from me?"

Peter looked around, ensuring they were alone. "Mara told me what you did. She said you're different and might be willing to help me too."

Tim furrowed his brow. "Help you with what? I don't even know what's going on here."

Peter sighed. "The northern sector is a testing ground. The government is experimenting with new technology, dangerous technology that could change everything. Mara was trying to gather evidence to expose the truth."

Tim felt anger and confusion. "I've already done enough; what more do you want from me?"

Peter's eyes hardened. "Those who know too much disappear. This isn't just about breaking the rules; it's about survival. Mara trusted you because she saw something in you. She believed you could tell the difference between right and wrong."

Tim's guilt deepened. "I let her through without knowing all the details. And I risked being found out for what I did. How do I know you're not an informant?"

Peter stepped closer, his face serious. "You did the right thing, Tim. And you can still help. We need someone on the inside to let a few more people through to support Mara."

Tim felt the weight of the decision. He wanted to help, but the fear of punishment and the uncertainty of trust made it difficult. "I don't know if I can do it," he admitted, barely audible.

Peter put his hand on Tim's shoulder. "You must have realized by now that the system is flawed, and we need people like you to help fix it. I'll be in the line tomorrow, and I ask that you let me through. I'll have all the papers and the number, too... but I know the Heine travelers are being watched even more closely now."

Tim nodded, feeling a faint determination. "I'll think about it."

As he stepped back into his apartment, the dim lights of the village casting long shadows on the sidewalk, Tim felt a surge of conflicting emotions. His inner turmoil was far from over, but he knew he couldn't turn a blind eye to the truth any longer. Mara's mission was more significant than he had initially realized, and his role in it was just beginning to unfold.

Tim sat down at his desk at his apartment and quickly immersed himself in his pending tasks. However, his thoughts were far away. He was still afraid and confident, but he knew that he could not return to blindly following orders. He was no longer the naive gatekeeper he had been.

In the morning, he was awakened by a loud knock, surprised by Judith's unusually early visit. His boss wasn't alone; she arrived with two young men in uniform.

"These are the two inspector friends who will be staying with you," Judith began, not waiting for Tim to invite them in, stepping into the room. "There's plenty of space, as I see, but we'll need to bring in some furniture."

Tim stood uncertainly, still groggy from the previous day's events. Then he gathered himself and greeted his two future roommates, who he realized he could do nothing to avoid, and offered them coffee.

"I don't need any, thanks; I have many things to take care of. But I'll leave you here, have your coffee, and then come up to the teleporter with Tim," Judith replied, still assessing the room to see how much furniture was needed.

Tim's sparse furnishings could use an update, but he had no illusions; he suspected they'd bring in some used furniture, junk from the city.

Pluto and Jamie placed their bags on the floor, as there was nowhere else to put them. The room had only a desk with a chair, a bed, and a wardrobe. A long shelf unit stood alone against one of the empty walls, but Tim didn't use it; it stood empty, merely filling space.

"So, you're the gatekeeper here?" the taller one, Jamie, tried to befriend him. "How many people usually cross in a day?"

Tim answered the questions, albeit reluctantly. He was busy making coffee and wondering if he should also offer them breakfast. Then he decided to keep things brief, showered, dressed, and headed to the gate. Noir also had two people staying with him, who joined Tim when they saw they were ready to go.

Tim was bombarded with questions; they wanted to know everything about how he did his job and how long it took to complete tasks. This made him uncomfortable. After all, they were inspectors; what else could he expect? He just hoped that it wasn't primarily him being inspected but the travelers. Then he thought of the figure from yesterday. How was he going to let him through?

Tim saw even more inspectors at the teleportation gate, distinguishable from the travelers by their blue uniforms, all standing and observing. This was unusual; plainclothes officers had been watching from the sidelines the day before.

Tim sensed the situation would be severe if such security measures had been taken. He only hoped that the person who had approached him the previous day wouldn't show up, seeing the tightened security and turning back instead.

The day began, and travelers stood in line, but everyone seemed much more anxious. Tim was busy with his work, but he noticed the inspectors occasionally calling travelers to present their papers and inquiring about their destinations. Suspicious individuals were pulled out of the line and subjected to lengthy questioning, increasing the nervous tension among the others—and in Tim.

After being questioned, the inspectors escorted some travelers away, who led them down the hill to an unknown destination. Tim tried to remain calm. He had some insight into the methods the inspectors used; besides coercion, they were authorized to use torture to uncover enemies of the state.

Tim wondered if he could skillfully maneuver and avoid these situations. In his naivety, he had previously thought that anyone who opposed authority deserved their fate. But Mara had shifted his worldview, leading him into this situation. He had let his thoughts wander again, and he had to remind himself to believe everything would be fine. Then Tim noticed the person from yesterday being pulled out of the line. He nearly fainted at the sight. After a long conversation, he saw one of the inspectors pushing the person down the hill from the corner of his eye.

Perhaps he was smart enough to say he was headed to a different city and didn't reveal his true destination? Although it didn't seem that way if he was being sent away. Tim felt a sense of relief because now he didn't have to decide whether to let him through or not. He had thought about what he would do, but the weight of the decision was so heavy that he kept pushing it away, hoping the person wouldn't show up or something would happen. And something did happen—they took him away. But now Tim is worried about what will happen next. Would the person tell them that Tim had already let someone through?

Then suddenly, he felt calm. He couldn't understand why. His nerves settled as the number of travelers dwindled and the number of inspectors decreased. The calmness that once characterized him began to return. For an outside observer, watching Tim take papers, study them, and enter codes into a device by the teleportation gate would make it seem like he was a robot. His movements were measured and calm. Nothing gave away the inner conflict raging inside him. No one saw that he felt like he was collapsing and that his limbs were trembling. This was why Judith considered him a good gatekeeper. Although his boss sometimes saw signs of him turning red, his posture, demeanor, and ability to maintain a professional tone reassured the leadership that Tim was a reliable and stable worker.

As Judith approached him, smiling, Tim was angry with himself for letting himself get stressed. There's nothing wrong here; if there were, he would have been taken away long ago, or someone would have been assigned to watch his every move.

"I'll walk you home, Tim. Let's talk on the way," said Judith, patiently waiting as he gathered his things.

The gatekeeper couldn't understand this sudden change, and deep in thought, he tried to force a smile on his face.

"I'm satisfied with your work! You've been doing an excellent job here. Even though quite a few people managed to get to Heine before the crackdown, none passed through this gate! That's something, Tim! You've earned the respect of the leadership as well. There will be a thank-you letter and a little bonus. You should be proud of yourself, and I am proud of you too because this is the only gate where no one passed through to Heine."

"Except for that woman, no one else wanted to go there, so it's not my doing!" Tim lowered his eyes, pondering the irony that he might receive a reward instead of punishment.

"Don't downplay your achievements; you're too modest. If any-one else had come, you would have resisted bribery, too. You're much more law-abiding!" Judith nudged him playfully.

Tim was surprised but said nothing, noting how peculiar this familiarity felt.

"I wanted to ask you, Tim, if you'd like to take a few days off, travel to the city, visit someone.

This was too much for Tim, and he even stopped in his tracks, so surprised was he. "Besides the mandatory vacations?"

"Yes, this is a kind of reward, but it's my little way of being nice to you."

"The thing is, I don't have anyone to visit. The people who raised me at the orphanage aren't there anymore; besides, I'm more tied to this place now."

"You've gotten pretty close to the cook!" Judith laughed.

"Can I ask you something?" Tim became serious. Without wait-ing for her response, he continued, "The people who were pulled out of the line today—was it random, a spot check?"

Judith was surprised by the question. "No, we had a list of those likely to travel in the coming days. The situation is getting worse, Tim. Everyone risks it because of the invention; once one person talks, an entire organization is exposed. Unfortunately, several groups are making excellent forgeries and even know how to hack the EPRS numbers."

Tim absentmindedly kicked stones along the road. "So, some-one in Heine got caught and ratted out the others?"

"Yeah, that's right. The authorithy revealed who provided the papers, and that person then protected themselves by giving up all the information. It was easy to unravel the entire network. It's simpler; no one can get in or out of Heine. It's completely closed off. Of course, some still try but mostly rely on bribery."

Tim was pleased with what he heard but wanted to know if he could ask more questions or when Judith might stop him from sharing confidential information. "And do you know anything about that girl who wanted to cross here? Did she cross elsewhere?" Tim felt he probably shouldn't have brought this up, but it was too late to take it back; the question slipped out so instinctively that he only realized his mistake when he heard his voice.

"No, she completely disappeared. Either she didn't cross, or she's hiding in Heine. But even if she did cross, she won't find peace because many soldiers have gone there, searching for her and others who don't belong in Heine."

Tim could already picture Mara's delicate face being beaten and her eventually revealing how she got through. He closed his eyes, but that made it even worse.

Chapter 6

S ignificant changes had occurred in his small house because the furniture had arrived, and someone had already set it up: two beds and two smaller wardrobes. A table with four chairs was placed in the middle. Tim was relatively silent during lunch; he didn't like that more and more strangers were arriving in the small village. But he also saw the worried looks of the locals, who were concerned that this might become permanent. Even Sara had more work now; she no longer served the food herself; a young girl was going around the tables instead.

Too many changes had occurred in just a few days. Tim had to get used to not being alone in his house anymore, which reminded him of the old days. When his two housemates arrived in the evening, he didn't know whether to be happy. He was partially pleased because they brought dinner and offered some to him. But beyond that, they wanted to talk, and Tim was too absorbed in his thoughts about Mara. He was too worried about the girl.

After finishing his mandatory tasks, he went outside into the yard to hear his thoughts. He stood in front of the scarecrow's junk again and only managed to lift some dusty pieces of clothing. Pluto also came out. He heard a deep, rumbling voice behind him:

"What are you planning to do with these?" the inspector asked curiously.

"I wanted to make a scarecrow because I planted corn behind the house," he gestured in that direction with his hand. "And if they sprout, I must scare the birds away. But I might be too late because the crows have gotten used to it; you can hear them cawing even now."

"If you want, I'll help. I don't have anything better to do."

Tim was surprised at how helpful he was, but he had to admit that the work went much easier this way, and the inspector boy had some perfect ideas and insights. By dusk, they had finished the crooked little scarecrow and were satisfied with their excellent job.

The next day, the gatekeeper was also greeted by changes at the teleport station. A pole had been dug into the ground in the middle of the hill, and a camera was mounted. Tim eyed the device suspiciously and looking around, he saw that it was the only one he could see. His two housemates didn't stand to the side but followed Tim and sat behind him. They watched his every move, or at least that was the feeling he got. Pluto noticed his discomfort and leaned closer to reassure him: "Relax, Tim, we're not monitoring you. The fuss is just because of the camera, to show that we're doing everything here!"

Tim felt somewhat reassured because he had almost thought someone would come and accompany him. Fewer travelers arrived, but those who did were much more thoroughly checked. His housemates also examined the papers and asked questions and other inspectors randomly checked travelers in the line.

This was all too much; he had yet to experience such strict checks in the city. Besides, he didn't understand why there was such a fuss about questioning travelers who weren't going to Heiné.

His previously routine job now felt like he was balancing on a tightrope, afraid of swaying to the right or left.

He didn't see Judith anywhere; he saw only the uniformed inspectors pulling people out of the line and leading them away.

Later, they walked together with the other inspectors towards the inn. For the first time, Tim realized just how angry the locals were. Their usual quiet life had been disrupted. Not only did Tim feel the change, but the locals also disliked the constant bustle, the comings and goings, and the many uniformed soldiers. This was clearly shown by the woman who, upon seeing them approaching, grabbed her child playing outside and ran into the house. Tim also saw people loudly slamming their doors shut elsewhere when they saw them coming. Tim couldn't understand why they expressed their anger this way.

At the inn, he faced another surprise. After lunch, everyone suddenly stood up, and champagne glasses appeared from somewhere. Holding one in her hand, Judith stepped forward and handed it to him: "Tim, I would like to convey the management's gratitude for how you perform your work and protect the teleport station from unauthorized crossings. We've chosen you as the employee of the month. Allow me to congratulate you!" She raised her glass high while the others received their champagne.

Tim took a big sip of champagne just as Judith mentioned the employee of the month title and successfully choked on it. The person next to him patted his back, and when he felt better and no longer needed to cough, he clinked glasses with everyone with his now-refilled glass and accepted the congratulations.

Sara had also prepared a cake, with a gray marzipan piece on top resembling a teleport station, which ended up on his plate along with the cook's smile. The chocolate cake was delicious, possibly with walnut pieces, but Tim didn't pay attention because he felt the whole situation was ridiculous and embarrassing. After the cake, he received a certificate with his name beautifully drawn and signed by two top officials. The employee of the month badge, which seemed small, somehow looked enormous in his hand. Judith saw how he was focusing on his palm, interpreting his distant gaze as profoundly moving. She took the badge from his hand and pinned it onto Tim's uniform.

She looked at her protégé proudly as if looking at her child since he could have been her son. "Well done, Tim, I'm proud of you! I know this gate will be in good hands when I leave. At least I won't have to worry about that!" she said gratefully, looking at Tim.

"Are you going back to the city?" Tim asked as he walked back to his house with Judith. It became a habit for his boss to accompany him home and then stop by Noir's place for a chat.

"As a matter of fact, I received a mission, an assignment. And although it's confidential, I still have to tell you because you'll have to let me through tomorrow," Judith said, glancing suspiciously at one of the locals who poured a bucket of water onto the road before them.

Tim paused. "You're going to Heine?"

Judith also stopped, but she gestured for Tim to continue walking. They both felt like the locals were watching them everywhere and giving them hostile looks. Judith even vocalized this: "What's gotten into everyone? When I arrived, not everyone was this hostile!"

"I think they don't like having their quiet lives disrupted... So, where do you need to go?" Tim insisted.

"Yes, there. It's quite a dangerous mission. We received a solid tip-off about who has the invention. I volunteered to retrieve it because I used to know one of the FYI members. Now I'll have the opportunity to interrogate him," Judith explained.

"I've heard of them, but what does FYI stand for? For your information?" Tim asked curiously.

"The official version, yes, but I think it's more like fuck you inquisitors, in my opinion... They'll do anything to undermine our existence, the inquisitors'," Judith grimaced.

"I never understood why they call the inspectors that. If I remember correctly, they used to call torturers that in ancient times," Tim pondered.

"Yeah, I believe you're thinking of the Spanish Inquisition, but this is different."

Tim wondered how this could be different since their methods were the same. Destroying the enemies of power at any cost.

"The girl who wanted to cross here, some Mara," Judith began, and Tim stumbled, even though the road was smooth. "She's also in Heine. She was identified, but there is no data in the system where she crossed."

"Wow!" Tim muttered.

"But it's only a matter of time before they catch her, so we don't need to worry about her. We're very close to unraveling the entire FYI organization in Heine and cleansing the place of them," Judith spoke passionately, showing her commitment to the authorities. And Tim felt like he used to be like that a few weeks ago, but then this girl came, and he started to think about things.

Suddenly, he thought, what if he told his boss he let Mara through? Would he be punished, or would they overlook his mistake? After all, he received an award today; it would look bad if the employee of the month made such a big mistake! But no, he couldn't do that to Judith; it would also be a failure for her.

"Traveling was always my dream," Tim said. "Maybe that's why I wanted to be a gatekeeper. I never thought about it, but gatekeepers don't travel anywhere; they just stand in one place. And they can only see the adventurous spirit of excited travelers. I envy you for being able to cross. I've always been curious about that island..."

"Well, I've been there once. It's a trendy vacation spot for the wealthy; you can imagine I wasn't there for a vacation... It has beautiful lagoons, and you can even take boat trips in the city. Quite lovely. But the real deal is not Heine; it's the smaller island next to it, Iop."

"Are there still vacationers there?"

"The rich society couldn't be banned, so this situation is complicated. Because permits were still being issued, costly permits that no one wanted to miss out on. But at least the local teleporters aren't working, so you have to swim from Heine to the little island. We've stationed guards on both shores, so the traffic is heavily monitored."

"That's why you said they'll catch Mara soon?"

"Sooner or later, yes," Judith said, and she was about to say goodbye to stop by Noir's place as usual, but Tim stood before her as if deeply contemplating something.

"Could you take me with you? As some sort of reward?" he blurted out, gathering his courage because he had been thinking about this for a while. This way, he'd have a chance to save Mara.

Judith was taken aback by Tim's determination. "How did you even think of that? This is a secret mission; I couldn't even tell you! And it's dangerous!"

Tim hesitated, but he felt more and more that he had to do this. "I was in the training for deployment, weapons handling, shooting, close combat. I excelled in all of them; you can look into it."

"I understand, Tim, but you've never been on a real mission. Learning the theory and going through the training courses is one thing, but a real mission is a bit different..." Judith seemed to be deep in thought.

"Judith, please. I'll never have another chance to leave this place. Let me go with you, let me practice, the real deployment. I could even be of help to you. I always knew I wanted to travel!" he pleaded with his boss, feeling like he needed a better reason: "I want to benefit you, catch the enemies of the authorities. And only I know what Mara looks like..."

"Hmm, interesting that you say that; we found an old recording of her... but that could also be a good reason. Let me think about it, Tim! In any case, I like how determined you are. I'll bring it up to the management, and then we'll discuss their decision in the morning."

They said goodbye, and Tim was glad that he still asked Judith despite his concerns, gathering courage. He didn't know exactly what he was doing but knew he didn't want to stand by the teleporter anymore.

With an unusual cheerfulness, he threw himself into his tasks, and he even had time in the evening when his inspector roommates arrived to welcome them with dinner. The two boys looked somewhat tired.

"What happened to you?" Tim inquired.

"It was quite a workload; today, we had to interrogate those whom we ejected from the queue yesterday and today," Pluto replied, and it was evident from his hand that it hurt; he kept rubbing it. Tim had no doubt about the nature of this challenging task, which must have been interrogation, but he didn't think they did it here in the village. He thought everyone was transported to the city.

"And was the work successful?" Tim asked as he cut bread for everyone.

"You know we can't answer that question. What's gotten into you?" Pluto took the bread and started eating.

Tim already regretted bringing it up; it was just a friendly conversation. He hoped he could leave soon because he also began to find the presence of the two inspectors oppressive. He knew how things worked in the system, but these had always seemed distant; now that he was part of the terrible things, he didn't like how things were going.

He entered the garden, looking at his cornfield with the scarecrow in the middle. Not a single seed had sprouted yet. Perhaps it was better because he knew he couldn't stay here after the day's happenings.

CHAPTER 7

The next day passed the same as usual. He felt a surge of excitement, and while checking the papers at the gate, he kept looking around to see if he could spot Judith anywhere. He didn't see her, and his anxiety only intensified. He was almost ready to calm down and talk out of his crazy plan, but he had time to think that day. Somehow, the number of travelers had dwindled, and there were just a few stragglers, with more inspectors than travelers. This way, they could practically check all the travelers, and they arrived at Tim already knowing all the data and destinations.

He thought of Noir, his trusted companion, with whom he had not spoken recently due to the past few days' events. They had missed their shared lunches and long silences. As he had more life experience, he was curious about how Noir saw things.

His two housemates were whispering behind him, and he involuntarily noticed that they were talking about the old man who spent all day sitting in the tavern. This was unusual for him, or maybe he was disturbed by the newcomers. Tim had adapted to them quickly, but he imagined how annoying it could be for an older person to have their routine disrupted.

With his mind wandering on various topics, the two hours passed quickly, but Judith still needed to be seen. He had only been to the tavern long ago, not since he was new and wanted to fit in. But Tim saw that the locals weren't amiable, treating even Noir, who had lived among them for decades, as outsiders. He also noticed that they ostracized their cook because they were friends. As he walks towards the tavern, Judith comes towards him.

"Tim, it's great that we ran into each other! I just got back from the city, and I have good news, you can come with me!" Judith seemed genuinely pleased about this. Tim, however, didn't know what to think anymore.

"Oh, I'm glad. When are we going?" Tim asked, somewhat surprised by the outcome. What did he expect? That it wouldn't be this easy? Yes, he was actually thinking about how to cross illegally, a thought that filled him with guilt and conflict.

"I need to find someone to take your place. I hope one of the two guys staying with you will take the job," Judith rambled on. "There's one more thing: I can officially take you with me as an inspector apprentice. If you successfully complete this mission, you'll be permanently assigned. So congratulations, Tim, this is actually a promotion for you." Judith patted him on the shoulder kindly.

The gatekeeper was speechless. He wanted this at some point; after all, everyone aspires to a better position, recognition, and climbing the ranks. The funny thing was that it happened when he became uncertain about the system and the rules. What would this new role entail? How would it change him?

"I see you're speechless! I'll go find your housemates, and then we'll have lunch together!" his boss said goodbye.

Tim wondered how Judith would sell the lower-ranking gatekeeper job to his inspector housemates. But that was not his problem anymore.

The tavern was right in the middle of the village, and from afar, he could see its winding tower. It was quite a unique building as if it were built as a castle, entirely out of place with the village's simple atmosphere. It was like someone had whimsically decided to surprise the town with an old building because it was clearly not old, as evidenced by the walls and floor. A new castle, this is what they call kitsch. The plastic animals and garden gnomes in the garden starkly contrasted the tavern's image.

Upon entering the tavern, the kitschy atmosphere disappeared, giving way to a severe ambiance dominated by dark wood and stone colors. Noir was sitting alone in a corner with a beer in hand. When he saw Tim, he forced a smile, clearly having already had a few pints. He also motioned to the bartender to bring a beer for the newcomer. Tim gestured that he didn't want one, but the waiter was already on his way with two beers.

Noir sat absorbed in his thoughts. The gatekeeper was used to sitting silently beside him, as the old man spoke only when he had something to say. He didn't like long, meaningless conversations. So Tim broke the silence. "I'm going to Heine with Judith."

Noir nodded and took out his pipe. He knew he couldn't light it here, but he still began to fill it, preparing it.

"If you asked me why," Tim continued, "I couldn't say. Well, there is an official reason: I've been promoted to inspector, and Judith has a mission that I'm accompanying her on."

Noir continued fiddling with his pipe, his trembling fingers scattering tobacco everywhere on the table. Tim reached out to help, but the old man pushed his hand away. Tim was surprised by this. "Actually, it's because of the girl. You know, the one who tried to bribe me. Somehow, she captivated me, and I couldn't get her out of my head. Has that ever happened to you?"

Noir now looked up from his concentration and scrutinized Tim for a long moment. "You're mixing things up. That's not good. Becoming an inspector is a serious matter, but your mind is on a girl who, if you think about it, is someone you'll probably have to hunt down?" He began to shake his head.

Tim realized this didn't make much sense, but if he could tell the old man everything, his greatest desire would be to see the girl again and save her. He didn't even know how to do it himself.

"Do you know what inspectors do?" Noir asked.

"They enforce the law..." Tim began to stammer but stopped abruptly because he knew what was coming.

"Yes, yes, the standard line. But do you know what the authority mean? At what cost?" The old man was no longer focusing on his pipe but was looking intently at Tim. "Are you sure you're ready for this? I know you. You have a gentle soul; you strive for good. I think you were born to be a gatekeeper. An inspector is a different thing. You're not like them. They're mercenaries." He whispered the last sentence closer so the few other patrons wouldn't hear.

Tim took a big gulp of his beer. He savored it, but he didn't like it. Nor did he like what the old man had said. He reconsidered what he was getting himself into. Not at all. "Noir, but if we look at our goal, this gatekeeper life, the next level is the inspectorate. If progress, advancement is our goal," Tim said, but he knew it wasn't a strong argument.

"Well, if that's your goal, you're on the right track! Judith is quite impressed with you. You have a good chance of getting into the leadership. If that's your goal..."

"Didn't you ever want more? You've been here your whole life, at this gate, and the locals haven't even accepted you!" He pointed towards the other patrons sitting at a table, with Noir sitting separately.

Noir returned to preparing his pipe and replied almost inaudibly. "It depends on what your goal is. I just wanted a peaceful life. Don't think that I didn't have ambition in my youth! I did, very much so. And I did some nasty things to get ahead. I betrayed my best friend and lied just to be chosen. And for a few months, I was an inspector, but I couldn't even look at myself in the mirror."

Tim was surprised because he couldn't imagine anything wrong with the old man. "You must have just made that up! I can't believe you'd be capable of anything bad!" Tim insisted.

"People are capable of surprising things when they believe what they are doing is good for them, especially when the law is on their side!" The old man had finished with his pipe and drank his beer. He was getting ready to leave, wanting to light up. Tim drank his beer, too, but not ultimately; he needed help to finish it.

Outside, Noir lit his pipe, and they slowly walked towards the hostel to have lunch. "Take care, Tim! Don't let them break your spirit! I think you know what's right and wrong. But be careful because evil can sometimes come in disguise. You might not recognize it, but consider the consequences."

Tim walked in silence, unsure of what to say. He couldn't tell him everything, but he was touched by Noir's concern for him.

The afternoon was mostly spent preparing. Tim thought he would get a uniform, but his boss brought street clothes instead; they needed to blend in. She didn't want to discuss the details of the mission, only mentioning that they would need to swim at some point.

At night, he had that strange dream again. He stood in a swampy forest, knee-deep in water, and Mara appeared again. This time, she grabbed Tim's hand, pulling him along. Tim quickly stepped out of the mud he had been stuck in and followed the girl, and together, they moved forward.

The following day, still under the influence of the dream, he barely noticed the world around him and didn't even pay attention to who eventually took over his post. He only realized he was standing at the gate with Judith as if they were regular travelers. He wore a ridiculous pair of shorts with colorful palm trees hanging loosely on his skinny legs, and he already hated the excursion. He couldn't understand why he had to wear shorts when the shirt Judith brought was long-sleeved. Then he realized they couldn't find the right size for him quickly. On the other hand, Judith was dressed nicely in a one-piece dress with a straw hat, looking ready for a vacation.

They both had rolling suitcases, but they were just for show, as there was nothing in them. Tim didn't even have time to get nervous or think about what was happening to him because he was suddenly standing in front of the gate and stepping into the blue light. Then he felt himself falling and again felt the ground beneath his feet. He found himself in a completely different world when the blue light disappeared.

Heine, where the sky was entirely blue without a cloud in sight, and the sudden heat and humidity hit him so hard that he felt dizzy. He felt his shirt getting wet under his arms. Someone grabbed his arm to help him move, and as he squinted to take in all the beauty around him, Judith appeared next to him.

The buildings were regal, with ornate details, gilded facades, and golden statues. Everything spoke of luxury and wealth, which is why this place was called the paradise of the rich. Tim felt out of place in this environment. Uncertainly, he followed his boss, who grabbed his arm and whispered, "Try to act like you're on vacation! Looking around is fine, but that look of despair on your face is not!"

Tim tried to muster some strength and force a smile. The trees were blooming everywhere, which was strange; they couldn't be accurate since it wasn't even spring. Do they even have seasons here? The weather was pleasantly warm, not scorching, just too humid.

The streets were spotlessly clean, and everywhere, people were taking photos, sitting on café terraces, enjoying their time, and vacationing. There were streets where water flowed, with gondoliers ferrying people around and bridges crossing over them. Tim couldn't stop marveling at the sights he had only seen in pictures or heard about. It was a clear sign that there was not only poverty in the world but incredible luxury, too, and Tim had never experienced this before.

Judith said their hotel was not the most expensive; it was one of the lower categories, yet it exceeded all of Tim's expectations. The bed had silk covers, and there was a private bathroom. He bathed for over half an hour, pouring fragrant oils into the water. He enjoyed this luxury, and by the afternoon, he felt so at home, as if he had always lived there. Judith still hadn't revealed anything about their mission, and she disappeared, instructing Tim to stay in his room.

He ordered lunch and then a snack, which he consumed on the balcony. He felt good and no longer regretted embarking on this adventure. All his doubts and thoughts about Mara seemed to have stayed behind in his old life in Walnut Grove.

From the balcony, he watched the many tourists pleasantly, imagining himself in their place, trying to figure out where they might be from, who they might be, and their relationships.

From his room's balcony, he could get an even better look at the blooming trees, which he had previously suspected weren't real, and now he was utterly convinced of it. He saw a gardener carefully cleaning the flowers and leaves with a cloth. At first, he found it amusing, and then he listened to the buzz of insects or birds chirping, but there was nothing like that. Just the noise of people bustling around and the distant roar of the ocean. He knew it wasn't every day he could see the sea, so Tim decided to go see it before Judith appeared, and they had to focus on the mission.

The receptionist gave him a map and kindly directed him to the sandy beach. He also rented a bicycle to return quickly and avoid his boss discovering he had left the room against her orders.

He hadn't ridden a bike since childhood, but they say you never forget how. After some awkwardness, he got the hang of it and rode down a steep slope, extending his legs to the sides. He felt like a kid again.

The beach and the ocean were lovely. He removed his shoes and waded into his knees; the water pleasantly tickled his feet, and the sand felt good around his toes.

Everything was beautiful, and watching the happy laughter of the bathers, he didn't notice the drones flying overhead at first. One stopped above him, and he became aware of it only then. He was caught; he wasn't supposed to be here and would have to explain himself to his boss.

Feeling defeated, he returned to the bicycle and pushed it uphill. On the way back, he paid more attention to the cameras. There were one everywhere—or two, or five on a single pole.

The surveillance was very effective here, and he had forgotten this feeling. There were none in Walnut Grove, so he had to get used to them again. Of course, if you live like this for a long time, you forget they're there, and every move is documented.

Okay, he had defied his boss's instructions. Would there be consequences?

CHAPTER 8

When Judith returned to the hotel room, she didn't look cheerful. Tim wasn't cheerful either because he was worried that his boss would find out that he had behaved like a disobedient child, leaving the hotel room despite his boss's orders. The assignment they were on was a high-stakes mission, and any deviation from their boss's instructions could have serious consequences.

Judith sat grumpily on her bed, a bit away from Tim's, separated by an armchair. She didn't even say hello; she was lying on her back in bed with her clothes on. When Tim tried to make a sound, clearing his throat, she didn't react. Tim got up and approached her to see if something was wrong, but he immediately smelled alcohol, which surprised him. Tim had never seen her like this and, secretly, was somewhat pleased by this turn of events because it stripped away a facade he had likely attributed to his boss. Maybe she wasn't as fearsome and unapproachable as he had thought, and this vulnerability made her more human to him.

It was late, and he didn't want to wake her, so he carefully draped a blanket over her. But when she felt this, she suddenly sat up, looked around, stared into Tim's astonished eyes, and then, as if understanding everything, lay back down, throwing the blanket off. Later, she even started snoring. This was too much for Tim, so he went to the balcony with his blanket and a small pillow, pushed two relatively comfortable chairs together, and decided to sleep there. The snoring and the smell of alcohol were too disturbing for him.

Surprisingly, he felt very comfortable on the balcony. It wasn't cold, and the city was still bustling, with people walking and chatting below. This pleasant background noise lulled Tim into a deep sleep, and he couldn't remember when he had slept so well. And fortunately, he didn't dream at all, waking up to the cool morning breeze feeling as if he had slept for a thousand years.

As the morning dawned, Tim was greeted by an eerie silence. No birds chirping, no frogs croaking, no buzzing of insects. Just an unsettling quiet. The tranquility was shattered by the soft hum of a drone, its presence jarring in the stillness. Tim's gaze was drawn to it, his unease growing. Was someone watching them? He resisted the urge to throw his small pillow at the buzzing device and decided to retreat indoors.

Judith was still snoring, so he went to shower. As he looked at his lanky face in the mirror, preparing to shave, he wondered what he was actually doing. Mara came to his mind, her sweet little face watching him, and he remembered the moment he missed the kiss and regretted not having the courage.

His electric shaver suddenly stopped as he pondered and drifted into his thoughts. It was charged, but it was useless no matter how much he pressed the buttons. With his face half-shaved, he started rummaging through the hotel toiletry cabinet and found a disposable pink plastic razor. He unwrapped it and turned it over in his hand. It was undoubtedly a woman's razor, but he had no choice.

Unfortunately, he cut himself a few times and had to put tissue paper on the wounds to stop the bleeding. He looked fantastic, with three minor cuts on one cheek.

Tim's stomach rumbled, a reminder of his hunger. He was eager to start the day, but without knowing Judith's plan, he felt a sense of anticipation. He decided to head down for breakfast, hoping that Judith would join him soon and reveal their next move.

It was already past ten when Judith appeared in the hotel dining room, a cup of coffee in her hand, and sat down in front of Tim wearing sunglasses. "Yesterday didn't go so well for me... I have a terrible headache." She took a big sip of her coffee and immediately spit it back into the cup. "This is completely cold!" She lifted the cup and looked around to catch a waiter's or someone's attention. A young boy came forward and took the cup. "Shall I heat it up?" he asked kindly.

"Could you bring a new one, please?" Judith asked. The boy nodded obligingly, but Tim had his doubts. Would he really bring a new one? And where did Judith get that coffee from anyway? She had come in with the cup already in her hand.

"I still don't feel well, and I'll tell you everything soon. The main thing is, today we're going to meet my contact, who gave me the assignment. I'll introduce you to him." Tim had been waiting for this since yesterday. He was eager to meet the person who had given them this important assignment, hoping to gain some insight into the mission and his role in it.

Tim was excited but didn't want to bring it up or rush things; instead, he passively endured Judith's scrutinizing gaze. "You look quite a sight... what happened to you?"

"Oh, this? Nothing, my shaver broke, and I found a disposable one among the toiletries."

Judith shook her head. "That wasn't your best decision. It would have been better if you'd come with stubble." Just then, the waiter reappeared with a steaming cup of coffee. Judith eagerly took a sip, but of course, it was too hot, and she hissed as it burned her mouth.

"Let's go!" Judith said, pushing her sunglasses up onto her head.

She confidently approached a small two-seater electric car parked at the hotel entrance. It was so tiny that Tim, being a tall man, felt uncomfortable, hugging his back and lowering his head a bit. On the way, Tim mostly looked around, observing the buildings and the majestic statues, while Judith remained silent. They had been driving for a while when the buildings started to thin out as if they were leaving the luxurious city center. The blocks of flats became more frequent, the kind Tim used to live in, and Judith finally parked in front of one of these. But she didn't get out; instead, she turned to Tim. "The person we're meeting now is our liaison with Zack. I was with him yesterday, and we had a bit of a disagreement. We've known each other for a long time. I wouldn't say we've settled our issues, but if you sense any tension between us, that's why. I'm telling you this because we have some fundamental disagreements."

Tim was curious about these fundamental disagreements, but his boss fell silent again. It seemed she had to work hard to get out of the small car. Was it just her hangover making her move so uncertainly?

They didn't enter the block of flats but went around it. Attached to the side of the block was a small shack, a one-room place, and as soon as they entered the shabby hovel, the smell of alcohol hit Tim here as well.

As he stood there uncertainly, he suddenly remembered what Judith had said. "Did you say Zack?" he leaned closer to her. "The head of the authorities? He's the one who hired us?"

Judith nodded. "Max, are you here?"

Due to the semi-darkness in the room, their eyes only slowly adjusted to the lighting conditions. When something moved and wobbled towards them, they identified it as a person, and both looked in that direction expectantly. A light turned on, and a small nightstand lamp illuminated only half of the figure sitting in the nearby armchair.

Max didn't stand up but stared at them suspiciously, mainly sizing up Tim. Judith broke the silence. "As I mentioned, I trust Tim. You can tell him everything. I haven't told him much about you yet."

The figure gestured towards the sofa opposite, with a blanket and pillow haphazardly placed, indicating it served as his bed. Judith tossed the blanket aside to make room for them, and they sat down.

"So, you haven't told him who I am?" asked Zack, taking a can of beer from the cooler beside him. "Want some?" he offered, but they both shook their heads, so he continued. "I'm the undercover guy who betrays everyone..." he laughed, then took a swig of his beer.

Judith took over the conversation. "Max knows the local groups and is on good terms with FYI. From them, we know that the new invention, the actual prototype, might be sold to them. Because the inventor, Bernard, is selling the invention's description to the authorities, the crucial task is to acquire the prototype to prevent it from falling into the hands of the resistance group."

Max shifted in his seat and leaned closer. "It's almost certain that the prototype has already been sold and bought directly from the inventor, which is odd since Zack and Bernard know each other well, and so far, the inventor hasn't shown any inclination to waver. But we need to confirm whether the teleportation device is with this group."

"So, that's the mission," Judith continued, "to retrieve the teleporter and bring it to Zack."

"I still don't understand why you're so determined to undertake this mission," Max objected. "And why do you have to bring a complete novice with you? I'd rather go alone..."

Judith shook her head. "We've already discussed this. Zack also believes that we need new people whom the group members don't know. Local inspectors aren't an option. And no one has come over from Tim's area."

Tim pressed his lips together, choosing to stay silent. He wondered about someone who knew him and what the consequences might be if Mara wasn't the girl he thought she was. What if she exposed him? He barely paid attention to the rest of the conversation, hearing it only as a murmur, lost in his thoughts. He knew he was doing crazy things.

Max suddenly stood up. "Alright, it's your call!" he said, heading over to his coat and hanging it on a hook Tim had only noticed. He fished a piece of paper from his pocket and handed it to Judith. "Here's the address. Go there. If they have the prototype, it'll be there. Take weapons; you might need them."

In the small car, Judith surprisingly became talkative. Tim wondered whether he should tell Judith about his adventure with Mara, just as it had happened. As he wrestled with this decision, he listened to Judith.

"So, Max and I were a couple once, but our convictions and worldviews didn't align. He was a full-fledged member of FYI for a while, and we have yet to hear from him during that time. In the past few years, he's been working like this, a bit here, a bit there. Of course, he sells the information for good money, which I also disagree with..."

"Isn't it dangerous then? How can we be sure he's giving us good info?" Tim asked worriedly.

"Others have thought of that, too. But I know he wouldn't deceive me. He promised me once, and I know he keeps his word. And you understand now why I was given the assignment. He only told me about the prototype thing... Of course, besides money, I also had to give him some info."

"So, you're a double agent too?" Tim asked, astonished.

"Not exactly. I'm not. I just give Max partial information, so he has something."

"But that's still called double-dealing! You're playing both sides!" Tim insisted.

"No! A double agent infiltrates the enemy; I don't. They don't even know who I am. I'm more of an informant if you want to label it. But above all, I'm an inspector leader."

Tim needed to be convinced that Judith fully understood the insignificance of her own role. To him, aside from the incident with Mara, an inspector's role was to ultimately serve the authorities. This didn't align with providing the enemy with some information.

"You can swim, right?" Judith asked as they drove into the center of Heine, evident by the luxurious decorations on the buildings.

"I can, yes. Why?" Tim asked.

"There's a small island not far away, Iop, where Bernard's lab is located, and the address we received is there, too. Unfortunately, it's well-guarded now to prevent anyone from the outside world from entering or leaving. But everyone who matters has gathered there. The FYI group and, as I understand, Zack are already there because of the invention."

"So, how do we get there?" Tim's legs were beginning to feel numb.

"By swimming. Teleporting is impossible, even for us, because it's completely sealed off. Boats are also not an option, as the traffic is monitored. There's one place where no one is watching, but due to the terrain, using a boat isn't possible either, so swimming is the only option."

Tim thought about how he vaguely remembered swimming, but that was during his childhood. "Can I practice swimming? It's been a long time since I've done it. Can I go down to the shore and swim a bit?"

Judith smiled as she got out of the car. "I was informed that you went out against my orders yesterday. And I'm not trying to encourage you with this, but you have a certain boldness that one wouldn't expect from you. Maybe that's why I think you'll make a good inspector... yes, you can go, but only for an hour, and I have to log the time you'll be out."

Tim regretfully trailed beside his boss. "I hope I didn't cause any trouble with yesterday..."

"Yes, you did. I told them I forgot to mention it, so next time, let me know, and I can handle it officially. Sleeping on the balcony isn't allowed either..."

"Well, the fresh air was nice..." Tim stammered, not thinking he could get in trouble for that, too.

"Look, Tim, you need to understand something," Judith said seriously as they entered their room. This place is for wealthy tourists to spend their money. You don't belong here, and you can't do as you please. For us to be left alone, the authorities need to know our every move so that they don't mistake us for unauthorized intruders."

Tim began to understand what Judith had said earlier—that if Mara had come over, they would catch her anyway. How had she managed to slip away or avoid the cameras and drones every-where?

Chapter 9

Tim was proud of himself for being granted permission to act like a tourist. He rented a lounge chair, sipped on some blue cocktail, and swam in the sparkling blue water. For almost an hour, he felt so carefree that he nearly forgot everything else. The drone didn't come as close to him as it had the previous day. He envied the other tourists who spent their days in blissful idleness. He longed for such a life. But he wasn't used to sunbathing and could feel his skin burning and turning bright red while still on the beach.

At night, he couldn't sleep on the balcony, had to listen to Judith's snoring, and barely dared to move because his skin hurt when it touched his clothes. Following Judith's advice, they applied something to his skin, which only temporarily eased the pain.

He woke up tired and in a bad mood, standing in front of the small car, wondering how he would squeeze into the tiny seat. He felt like he had lost his zest for life. Fortunately, they didn't have to endure the discomfort of the little vehicle for long. As they followed the coast, they turned onto a small road leading up to the cliffs.

"We have to walk a bit here," Judith said, setting a brutal pace that had Tim, despite his long legs, almost jogging to keep up. They maneuvered over rocks, and it became clear why the authority wasn't monitoring this area. Although the view from above was breathtaking, it was dangerous too. The sea was beautiful, and a tiny island with a sandy beach and palm trees wasn't far away. The little houses with red roofs were visible from this distance. Where they planned to swim from could have been more friendly; they had to jump from a high cliff into the water.

Judith searched for a suitable spot to jump from for a long time. Tim sat down, suddenly realizing he had a bit of a fear of heights but didn't want to bother Judith with it. Tim already felt strange with his bright red face and shoulders, plus the cuts on his face from the day before. He didn't want to annoy further his boss, who was already angry at him. They had severe work, and he looked like a teenage boy preparing for his first date.

When Judith finally shouted that she had found a good spot, he clung to the protruding rocks, dizzy and barely daring to look down. His boss removed her shoes, tied the laces together, and hung them around her neck before throwing them over her back. He followed her example, using it as an excuse not to look down.

"I'll go first. Wait a bit before you jump. Then catch up with me so we can swim together. Is everything alright? You look so pale!" Judith worried as she stood at the very edge of the rock.

"Yeah," Tim groaned, fighting the nausea. Judith jumped, and Tim counted to ten, thinking he should go to the end of the rock. At ten, Tim took off and, without looking down, hurled himself into the void. The water was cold and salty, and he wasn't even aware of when he surfaced, but his mouth and eyes burned from the salt water.

It wasn't so bad once he got used to the icy water and found a breathing rhythm to avoid getting exhausted. With Judith swimming beside him, he felt safe. The waves were small, making the water pleasant, and they made steady progress. However, distances were deceiving; he started to tire, and the shore didn't seem to get any closer.

To the right was a tiny island, just big enough for three palm trees and nothing else. He saw Judith head in that direction. He was relieved she was tired, too, because his side was hurting from the exertion.

Resting felt good, but only for the first few minutes. The sun soon became relentless, and the palm trees offered little shade. They drank and prepared to get back in the water when Judith pointed out their direction. "Let's try to swim to the right, see that little cove? There, so we don't end up on the open beach."

When they finally reached the shore, Tim's feet sank into the soft sand, and he was using his last reserves of strength. He was utterly exhausted. "Will we have some time to rest?" he asked as he followed his boss through the bushes.

Judith stopped in a clearing. "We have a place to stay where we can change, and there should be clean clothes and food. But we need to hurry; we have work to do tonight!"

Tim wasn't pleased. As Judith put it, he would have preferred to act the next day, but he didn't want to whine like a baby.

On Iop Island, there were also vacationers, but it was much more luxurious and secluded. Tiny houses had large pools and extensive grounds. They sneaked through the gardens, and Tim felt Judith knew where to go. At one point, they came onto a paved road, but Judith decisively crossed it and returned to the bushes. Not following the road completely embarrassed Tim because he expected them to get to the house by now, but instead, he still had to go.

After a long detour, they reached the small hut, well-equipped with everything except food. Tim opened the fridges and cabinets, and there wasn't even a canwas of food left behind. However, there were clothes, toiletries, and plenty of alcohol.

After freshening up and choosing a modest gray T-shirt and jeans combination, Judith distributed the weapons. Each got a pistol, which they hid in their pants' waistbands, covered by their shirts.

Their stomachs growled louder and louder, so they decided to find a restaurant and eat before their mission. Fortunately, Judith didn't want to walk anymore. After a long search, she found a car key. They were happy there was a car, but they had to search for it first because there were three cars in the garage, none of which matched the key.

Judith didn't give up, constantly pressing the key, hoping the sensor wasn't working correctly. When they had almost lost hope, stepping out of the garage, a car beyond the fence—a jeep—chirped.

It was more spacious than Judith's previous car; Tim no longer had to worry about his head hitting the ceiling whenever the vehicle drove over a bump. They went through beautiful places, winding along serpentine roads that offered views down to the sea.

They then arrived in a small seaside town where vacationers were leisurely strolling around, exuding a sense of calm that made it hard for Tim to believe this island was also home to resistance teams, including the FYI. He was excited because he imagined Mara might be somewhere nearby.

He saw no cameras, not even in the little restaurant they entered. The place looked like a breakfast spot, with people sitting at the long counter drinking coffee and eating pastries or omelets.

Tim and Judith sat at a table by the window, and a waitress was immediately at their side, smiling as she poured coffee from a pot she carried. "Are you new around here?" she asked kindly, handing them two menus. She did all this so quickly and professionally that any suspicion Tim had about why she was asking such questions vanished. It helped that Maria—this was the name embroidered on her red apron—was so attentive and friendly.

"Maria, right?" Judith asked. The waitress nodded, so Judith continued. "What's the most filling meal you have? We're pretty hungry."

"Peter!" Maria called out, and a fuzzy figure popped his head out from the kitchen. "What?" shouted the cook.

"Do we still have any hamburger patties left?" Maria shouted back.

"Only one left!" the cook yelled, disappearing again.

"So, as you heard, we only have one hamburger left, but Peter can make you a ton of eggs with bacon and cheese. And we still have pie, but only rhubarb." The waitress looked at them expectantly, glancing from Judith to Tim, pencil at the ready to jot down their order.

Tim was engrossed in the menu, which listed many other items—steak, spaghetti, pizza—but it seemed they were out of these.

"So that's all you have? Eggs and one hamburger?" Judith asked, flipping through the menu.

"Yes, unfortunately, our supply didn't arrive this week. We usually get a large shipment on Wednesdays, but there's yet to be any sign of it. No one knows what happened to it. Haven't you heard about it?"

"I'll take that hamburger, and Tim will go for the eggs—how about six? And we'll also have two rhubarb pies," Judith said, closing the menu angrily.

Tim wasn't happy about having to eat eggs. Maria collected the menus from the table and sashayed away to place their order.

"She could have just shouted what we ordered," Judith said, watching Maria. "She's pretty, isn't she?" she asked Tim.

Tim was more interested in the other, somewhat peculiar patrons—at least, they seemed strange. An older lady was knitting, while the elderly gentleman she was with sat at the same table reading a book.

Looking around more closely, he noticed a bookshelf by the entrance. "Nice touch," he thought. But why weren't these people sunbathing on the beach or enjoying the cooling water of the pool at their vacation homes?

The people at the counter were also interesting, especially since they occasionally cast suspicious glances and whispered among themselves. "I don't like this place," Tim whispered to his boss.

"Oh, come on, don't be so stiff. If you act like that, you'll draw suspicion," Judith replied, raising her cup to indicate she wanted more coffee.

Maria appeared instantly, and as she refilled their cups, she tried again, "And what brings you to our lovely little town?"

Judith tried to be pleasant. "Just passing through, nothing special. But it is a charming town, and the people here are exceptionally nice."

Tim felt his stomach churn, unsure if it was due to hunger or his boss's sugary words. Knowing why they were there made him feel genuinely nauseous. He went to the restroom but only dry-heaved; he hadn't eaten anything all day, so there was nothing to vomit.

When he returned, Judith was about to take a huge bite of her hamburger. The thick sauce oozed out between the buns, mixing with the meat juices in an unappetizing mess. Tim couldn't take his eyes off Judith and her hamburger-eating technique. Although to an onlooker, it might have seemed impossible to compress the two buns and double patties into a bite-sized portion, Judith managed it, even though juice ran down her chin.

Tim glanced down at his plate. The scrambled eggs seemed like a joke compared to Judith's meal. He picked at them unenthusiastically and ate reluctantly.

They got engrossed in their meal—at least Judith did. They didn't notice four men entering and sitting behind them, all wearing jackets, which was quite suspicious in this heat. Judith only became aware of them because they sat behind Tim when one grabbed the other's neck, and a gun appeared.

Maria's commanding voice caused everyone's heart to skip a beat. "You know the rule! No weapons in the restaurant!" Her words were surprisingly effective as the man raised his hand and put his gun away. Though their conflict wasn't resolved, they glared at each other angrily.

Judith buried herself even deeper into her hamburger, seemingly intent on making a mess of herself. "You're right, Tim. This place is peculiar. We might have come to the wrong place."

Tim didn't understand Judith's words but suspected she was referring to the men behind him. He didn't want to turn around to look at them; he could tell from Judith's expression what kind of people they were.

After paying, they hurried through their pie and discussed the situation in the car.

"Who do you think they were?" Tim asked, guessing Judith didn't leave in such a hurry by chance.

"I think we met some of the FYI's heavy hitters. I hope they didn't figure out who we are," she replied, starting the car anxiously.

CHAPTER 10

They were driving towards the specified address, now with full stomachs. Tim wondered if telling Judith the story about Mara would be a good idea. He always feared that if someone discovered that Mara was here, they would immediately know who let her through, or maybe they already knew, and this was all just a test. It would be much clearer if he told Judith and had an ally who might understand.

He tried to steer the conversation toward a point where he could reveal his secret. While thinking about a good topic, he needed to pay more attention to Judith, who was still talking about Maria.

"Don't you think Maria was pretty, Tim?" Judith asked, gripping the steering wheel as they descended another winding road.

"Who?" Tim asked in surprise.

"For heaven's sake! What's wrong with you? Do you even have a type? An ideal woman? Didn't you notice how that poor waitress looked at you?"

Tim needed help understanding. The idea that a woman would notice him felt strange. "Uh, no. I think you're mistaken!"

"You're tall, handsome; girls go for tall guys!" Judith continued, but Tim needed to understand where his boss was going with this. He wanted to steer the conversation towards Mara instead.

"And what about you and Max? If I understand correctly, you're members of opposing groups, but you were a couple? How did you manage that?"

Judith's expression darkened. "Don't think I will tell you a Romeo and Juliet story. However, the opposing group part is true. But when the initial infatuation fades in everyday life, you're not as patient and understanding. We couldn't convince each other of our truths. He deeply despises authority and how it tries to control everything. I believe in rules. These extremist groups, who knows whose interests they represent? They could be anyone, and you buy into their catchy slogans."

"Did it never cross your mind to agree with him and join the resistance because of him?"

Judith looked at Tim, then quickly returned to the narrow road, watching for oncoming cars. If there were any, they had to pull over to the edge of the road, right where the cliff began. "Interesting question. Are you expecting me to say I was so in love that I even considered that? Don't expect such madness from me. I've always been much more practical. Maybe Max was the more in love one between us? But see, he didn't leave the resistance for me either. If you're thinking that we weren't truly in love with each other, is that your conclusion?"

Tim didn't know how to respond, and Judith continued: "Things aren't always just black and white. Maybe both of us were waiting for the other to make a decision. Then the years just passed by..."

"If you could go back in time, wouldn't you decide differently and join his side for his sake?"

"You've seen Max, haven't you? He became a drunken idiot with a confused worldview. The fact that we were really into each other is another story. Maybe even now, we love each other in our way, and the chemistry works between us, but is that enough for a happy relationship? I don't think so..."

Tim felt several times that it was the right moment to confess what he had done for Mara, but then he changed his mind. Judith wouldn't understand the situation, and she might even discourage him, or who knows what she would do to Mara.

They arrived in another small fishing village and parked further from the house. "This must be it," Judith said, getting out of the car. Tim watched as she loaded more bullets into her pockets and even handed him a few.

"Do we have a plan?" Tim asked.

"I'll do the talking. You just keep an eye on them, and if anyone reaches for a weapon, shoot immediately," Judith instructed. "Can you handle that?"

"Sure!" Tim replied, following his boss, who decisively went around the house, aiming to enter from behind. There, they needed to climb over the fence.

They were lucky because there was a terrace at the back, and its door was open. What a recklessness, thought Tim.

They entered the kitchen, where a bluish light filtered in from the living room. A bag of chips lay open on the kitchen counter, and Judith reached in and took one, eating it as if it were the most natural thing in the world.

As they stepped into the living room, they saw two people playing a video game on a giant TV while a third person occasionally glanced at them from the table and read something. Judith signaled Tim to keep an eye on the gamers while she approached the one at the table, pressing her gun to his head.

All three reacted instantly. The two gamers stared at Tim, who aimed alternately from one to other, while Judith calmly sat on the table, still holding the gun to the seated man's head. "What are you reading?" she asked, taking the book from his hand. "The Hitchhiker's Guide to the Galaxy is an excellent choice!" She tossed the book back onto the table. "I read it once, but I have to admit, I don't remember much. The premise is genius, and the answer to everything is brilliant, but the story gets a bit messy towards the end, doesn't it?"

The man at the table gasped for breath, looking between Tim and Judith.

"Am I right?" Judith asked.

"What?" the man replied as if he didn't know where he was.

"Focus on me a bit. You're Donald, right?" Judith asked as if she weren't holding a gun but chatting casually.

The man nodded, now entirely focused on Judith. "So, Donald. You have something that belongs to Zack. Do you know what it is?"

Donald lost control again, looking around frantically. Judith didn't like this. "I said, focus on me! We'll be out of here if you tell me where it is. If not, and we have to find it ourselves, I might get a bit crankier, and you might not be useful to us. After all, we can find it on our own."

Donald nodded and looked towards the kitchen cabinet.

"Will you check the kitchen cabinet? I'll keep an eye on these guys here."

Tim cautiously backed away and disappeared into the kitchen while Judith kept the gun on Donald and didn't take her eyes off the other two.

"Got it?" she asked when she no longer heard the cabinet doors banging.

"Uh-huh!" Tim shouted.

Then Tim appeared with a small black briefcase, which he opened to show Judith, who nodded in satisfaction. Tim closed the suitcase and held it in one hand while holding his gun with the other, returning to his previous position.

"Gentlemen! Thank you very much for your cooperation. I hope you don't mind if we take our leave now!" Judith said, lowering her legs from the table to the floor.

Donald seized this moment of distraction, grabbing Judith's hand and trying to wrest the gun from her by pushing it upwards.

Tim watched the scene nervously, aiming his gun at the other two to ensure they wouldn't dare move. However, they were also waiting for the right moment, and one of them suddenly pulled out a gun and aimed it at Tim.

Now, they were both aiming their guns at each other while Judith and Donald were still grappling to control Judith's weapon. No longer under surveillance, the third person jumped up and disappeared through a door.

"Leonard!" shouted the man who was staring down Tim.

Judith was starting to lose the struggle, and with an unfortunate maneuver, Donald knelt and aimed the captured gun at the prone Judith, pulling the trigger. Or rather, he tried to, but the weapon clicked and didn't fire, as if it had jammed.

At the same time, Tim assessed the situation and realized he had no choice but to use his gun. He first shot the man standing and then Donald, who was momentarily distracted by the malfunctioning weapon.

His aim was surprisingly accurate. Judith jumped up and picked up her gun from the floor to see if it didn't work. She fired a shot at Donald, and it worked for her.

Standing there, they remembered the person who had entered the opposite door. Tim headed towards it just as the door burst open, and the man appeared with a gun, aiming directly at Judith. The bullet grazed her ear, but he had no time for another shot because Tim, standing right beside him, shot him dead.

Judith stood with a bloody hand pressed to her ear. "Let's get the hell out of here!" she commanded. But first, Judith grabbed a bunch of paper towels from the kitchen roll and wrapped them around her hand, covering it completely, and pressed them to her heavily bleeding ear. Then she reached for the bag of chips on the kitchen counter, taking the whole bag with her.

Tim just stood there, holding the door, waiting for Judith. His face showed his astonishment. "Really? You're taking the chips?"

Judith didn't answer, just nodded grimly. She looked angry and struggled to climb over the fence, hindered by the bloody paper wad in one hand and the bag of chips in the other, clutching them as if they were treasures. Tim sensed something was wrong, so he let her do what she wanted without saying more. He tried to help her jump down from the top of the fence by supporting her by the arm, but Judith impatiently brushed away his offered arm.

As they approached the car, Judith nervously avoided the driver's seat, handing the keys to Tim. "You got the briefcase, you shot them, you passed the test, damn it! You deserve to drive!"

Tim was curious if he should be happy. He tossed the briefcase onto the back seat and started the car. Judith ate chips and kept touching her ear.

"I've been thinking; it can't be a coincidence that the bullets meant for me missed twice!" Judith finally blurted out what was bothering her after she finished the entire bag of chips. She rolled down the window and threw out the empty bag.

Tim didn't like this behavior and shook his head. "Seriously? You just threw it out?" he scolded her.

At first, Judith didn't understand, then she resignedly said, "Alright, you're right. Stop the car!"

"Seriously? You want me to stop now?"

"Yes, damn it, stop!" Judith shouted.

Tim pulled over and backed up a bit to look for the bag. It was dark, and they couldn't see much on the roadside. "Maybe it flew into the woods," Tim speculated.

They exited the car and searched for the bag along the road. Tim sensed it wasn't about the bag; something else was behind Judith's strange behavior.

"So you think it was fate or something?" Tim tried to make conversation as they moved further from the car, even checking the other side of the road.

"Think about it; first, the gun jammed, and he pulled the trigger twice. Do you know what it felt like lying there, waiting helplessly for your brain to splatter? The weirdest things crossed my mind... your life does flash before your eyes. Then the second time, I was standing there, facing another gun, the same feeling all over again..." Judith stopped.

"We might have passed it if it had flown into the woods; that bag is light enough. Let's head back; we shouldn't leave the car unattended," Tim said, and they started walking back.

Judith continued her train of thought. "Tim, how could you shoot so calmly? Your hand didn't even tremble!"

Tim hesitated. "I don't know, I just did what you told me to..."

"What if I had come alone, as I originally planned? This whole thing is strange; I'm thinking it's a sign. The universe is warning me about something; it's fate. It feels like I still have something to do here. I don't know what." Judith looked up at the sky as if expecting an answer.

"I think it was just a coincidence, and you were fortunate," Tim replied.

"So you don't believe in fate?" Judith asked.

"If we saw every little event in our lives as fate, we'd be in big trouble. We'd constantly be looking for signs where there are none."

"But Tim, seriously, twice in a row, things worked out so that the bullet meant for me didn't reach me?"

"First, the gun jammed; it can happen anytime, and then it was just a matter of inches; yes, you were lucky. It's hard to aim precisely at someone's head, even from such a close range..."

Judith walked past the car towards the woods.

"Where are you going? Seriously, why is that bag so important?" Tim shouted after her.

"I saw something shiny over there; I think it's the bag; wait, I'll be right back," she replied, but she stopped after a few steps because they heard a gunshot.

CHAPTER 11

They heard five more gunshots coming directly from the forest before them. Tim thought the best thing would be to get into the car and continue the journey to Zack, so he turned to hurry back to the car.

However, Judith didn't move; she started walking towards the gunshots and disappeared among the trees, leaving Tim unable to see what was happening. Tim was trying to decide whether to follow his boss, worried about getting involved in something dangerous. When you hear gunshots in a forest, two things come to mind. Either hunters are shooting, and it's best to avoid wandering among the trees to prevent being mistaken for an animal, or there's some dirty business going on, like a showdown or something similar, and it's also not good to sneak around in the bushes in that case.

These thoughts crossed Tim's mind as he stood next to the car, sometimes taking a step as if he should see what was happening, then changing his mind.

Then he heard rustling from the forest and was relieved to think that Judith had returned, but to his surprise, a girl of about twelve came running out, looking terrified. When she saw Tim and the car, she stopped and stared at Tim with big brown eyes while Tim waited expectantly, watching for Judith to appear.

She did come, and as she ran, she grabbed the girl and continued running to the car, where she opened the back door and shoved her in. Then she quickly turned around and stood next to Tim. Before doing so, she signaled to the girl to crouch down.

Tim was catching his breath. "Not a word about the girl!" Judith whispered.

Tim didn't have long to ponder what had just happened when five men in suits and sunglasses emerged from the forest, clearly searching for someone and looking around frantically.

When they saw the odd pair, they aimed their weapons at them, but Judith seemed prepared for this. She raised her hand, showing her badge.

"She ran across the road that way," Judith pointed to the forest beyond. "But she was swift; we almost hit her."

One of the suited men came closer and inspected the badge, then looked at Judith's ear and shoulder, which were covered in blood. "Undercover? That is why you are not in uniform?" he asked, then signaled to the others to continue searching for the girl.

Tim tried to position himself to obscure the child hiding in the back seat with his shoulders, not fully understanding his urgency. He only knew he would be in trouble if they discovered they hid the girl. He was protecting his skin.

"Yes, we recovered something for Zack. But you guys are chasing a child?" Judith asked.

"Orders are orders. You know that," the man said, lighting a cigarette and offering one to Judith. "We had to finish off the entire family. Parents, child. Just because the father screwed up, really badly."

Judith nodded as if she grasped the issue. Then, the suited man took a deep drag from his cigarette, flicked it away, and waved at them in farewell before heading into the forest across the road.

They waited a bit longer until he disappeared, then got into the car.

Tim didn't say a word while Judith turned around and handed a water bottle to the sniffing child. "Stay down; everything will be alright!" she reassured.

"You've completely lost your mind!" Tim burst out.

"I know, but I couldn't do anything else. There are limits, after all! A child? That's too much!"

"You completely confuse me. You talk about rules all the time, and now you break them like it's nothing. And how long do you think it will take them to realize the girl is with us? They won't find her anywhere! We were right there with the car!" Tim shouted.

"They won't suspect us. That's why I mentioned Zack, to let them know we are trusted. Trusted people wouldn't do something this crazy!"

Tim fumed; his boss's explanation didn't convince him. "If you again start with your destiny... That's why you did it? You think it was all fate?"

Judith explained much more calmly. "Think it through, okay? Let's think it through. Why did we stop? Because of the chip bag. And do you know why I bought it? Because it was my favorite kind when I was a kid. My brother and I always fought over it, and I would hide to eat it without him seeing."

"You drive me nuts, seriously! It is all a coincidence! Got it? There was just that kind of chip; you wanted it, took it with you, and threw it out the window because you're a jerk!" Tim didn't care that he was talking to his boss and using such language; he was angry. "Then we stopped, and this happened right there."

"So, you're saying it was just a coincidence that I threw the bag out when a kid was in such trouble? Isn't it fate that we helped her?" Judith argued.

"And you took the chips because fate knew you'd throw them out? Admit it, this explanation is flimsy. It's a huge sequence of events, coincidences following each other."

"If we weren't there, this kid would be dead, Tim; you know that too!"

"No way; what if she was quick enough to escape them? She could have hidden well enough not to be found."

"And then? What would have happened to her? On an island where, even though there are no cameras, the authorities are everywhere and control everything. It would only be a matter of time before they found her!"

Tim didn't like the explanation; he was more concerned about what would happen next. "The authorities control everything, yet the resistance is here. All your explanation is beyond me. I can't follow..."

"You're right; let me rephrase. The authority tries to control everything. The resistance came because of the invention; if they get the teleportation devices and market them, everyone could teleport wherever they want, without any restrictions..." Judith replied.

"And what now? What do we do with her? Take her to our place? How do we get her off the island?" Tim bombarded her with questions as if he had already resigned himself to the fact that he was now an accomplice. He tried to think of a solution because he felt it was impossible to convince Judith that this wasn't all fate.

"I thought of someone who might be able to help us. Because we need fake papers as quickly as possible."

Tim suddenly stopped resisting because another problem occurred to him: Mara. This incident might solve her case, too.

The child had stopped sniffling in the back seat and was quietly observing, too scared to move. Judith occasionally glanced back to check if she was alright.

"So, that's the plan?" Tim resumed the conversation. "You know someone who can get fake papers?"

"Yeah, but we need to go further, into the mountains, where the Labs are. You know, the secret experiments, where they developed the little teleportation device."

"Who's our person? Some scientist?"

"More like a guard."

"Seriously, we're getting fake papers from an official? I thought you knew some underworld figure..." Tim said incredulously.

"I don't know what you imagine, Tim. Do you think the world is just black and white?" Judith asked.

"I hoped it was that simple, but everything is much more complicated. And what's your plan? We go there and ask for papers. Then what? How do you get her out? There aren't any teleporters anymore!"

Judith thought for a moment. "The person owes me, so I think he'll help. There's no teleportation to the island, but you saw if you have enough money, you can move freely as a tourist."

"I hate this double standard," Tim burst out. "If you have money, the rules don't apply to you... And you said you love rules, but we keep ending up with your acquaintances being informers or selling fake papers..."

"What's your point, Tim?"

"My point is that while you act like the model agent for the authorities, you follow your path and only the rules that suit you."

"That's quite a hasty statement, especially since you are in this situation just for a few days," Judith countered.

They entered the small fishing village where they had stayed but only stopped at the small gas station. Judith first went to the restroom to clean herself up, washing her ears, neck, and hands not to alarm the attendant. But it was futile, as the lady still stared at her.

"I fell," Judith explained and bought a T-shirt decorated with little pink palm trees and coconuts. She changed into the shirt right there, tossing the bloody one away. She also bought some sandwiches and water, and to be kind to the girl, she got a bar of chocolate.

They continued into the mountains, and after a sharp right turn, the sea disappeared from view, replaced by winding roads between huge rocks.

They stopped at one point, after driving for hours, to eat. The girl eyed them suspiciously but accepted the sandwich and chocolate. She sat on the ground to eat while the other two leaned against the car. Dawn was breaking, the dark sky giving way to light blue.

"What's your name?" Judith asked the child. The girl swallowed her bite and indicated her throat, showing she couldn't speak.

"Oh, alright. I'll get some paper to write me your name and your parents. I'll need them for the documents to get the ID card so we can get you out of here. Do you have any relatives somewhere?"

The girl nodded and continued eating.

"Is it good to mention her parents' names in the documents? And involving her relatives would be a big mistake. I have no idea what you plan to do with her..." Tim shook his head.

Judith didn't reply, lost in thought.

"I have some contacts, and I know where I'll send her, where she'll be safe. I'm more worried that we should have delivered the bag to Zack by morning. We need to come up with a good excuse for our delay."

In the mountains, the air was much more relaxed. They felt that their t-shirts weren't keeping them warm enough. The girl had fallen asleep in the back seat, and they could hear her steady breathing. Tim was glad because he couldn't imagine the horrors the child had endured. Watching her parents die and then driving off with two strangers to who knows where. Poor kid!

"Your ear looks pretty bad; shouldn't you disinfect it?" Tim worried.

"I forgot all about it!" Judith touched her ear. "When I went to the restroom at the gas station, I washed it a bit, but only superficially."

Tim felt it might be the right moment to talk about Mara. "I need to tell you something... because I did something..."

Judith watched him with interest, but the girl sat up and started gagging at that moment. She covered her mouth with her hand but couldn't hold it back, and Tim, startled, braked. The sudden motion caused the girl to slide forward and throw up between the two front seats.

"I have to change my clothes for the second time today!" Judith looked at the stain on her shirt as they exited the car. Tim looked just as splendid while the girl's clothes remained clean, but she had other issues: she was still leaning over the ditch and vomiting.

Judith's maternal instincts kicked in, and she approached the girl, holding her head and forehead while soothing her. Tim found a water bottle to bring to the girl and looked at the seat, wondering how they would clean up the mess.

"She doesn't look well," Judith shook her head. Now feeling better, the girl stood between them and began to cry. Tim didn't know what to do, so he handed her the water bottle, which Judith took, unscrewed the cap, kneeled in front of the girl, and comforted her. The girl suddenly hugged Judith's neck and sobbed.

Tim felt a bit useless, so he cleaned up the vomit, thinking he could only do it with his shirt since he had no other tools.

Tim, now shirtless, and the two girls in the back seat, leaning against each other, drove the final kilometers to the lab with the windows rolled down.

"Can your guy lend us some clothes? It's pretty cold around here," Tim grumbled. Judith directed him where to go, as they weren't heading to the main entrance but along a small dirt road towards Jim's little house. From a distance, they could see the white box-like buildings of the lab, surrounded by high wire fences.

After a while, the dirt road became so bumpy that they decided to walk. Tim couldn't believe his eyes when he realized the small forest they were walking through was full of walnut trees.

"What's the connection between walnut trees and teleporters? Or is it just a coincidence that there are so many walnut trees here?" he asked.

"Now that you mention it... I never noticed before. But you might know that Professor Walnut, the inventor of the teleportation system, had one of his forgotten experiments further developed here by Bernardt. Maybe they planted the trees in his honor. Who knows. But you might be right; it could be a coincidence," Judith softened as they arrived at a tinny house.

"How well do you know this, Jim? Will he be happy we drop by?" Tim asked, but there wasn't time to think about it as the small cabin door burst open, and a grumpy man appeared with a shotgun, wearing a loose robe and slippers. His grayish-blue robe flapped around him as he suddenly appeared, showing he had rushed out, not minding that the uninvited guests could see his funny avocado-printed underwear.

CHAPTER 12

J immy persistently aimed his shotgun at them, only lowering it when Judith stepped forward with her hands raised. "Come on, Jim, don't you recognize me?"

"Well, look who it is!" He stepped down the three steps, and they hugged. "You scared the hell out of me! Who's this half-dressed guy and the little girl? Where'd you find them?"

"It's a long story," Judith evaded. "We had a bit of an accident in the car, and we'd appreciate it if you could give us some clothes. I still have vomit dried on mine."

"I was wondering what that stench was!" Jim waved his hand in front of his nose.

He invited them into his clean, small house. Upon entering, Tim felt a bit uncomfortable as he was hit by the scent of flowers.

"Take off your shoes!" Jimmy commanded, and they dared not disobey. "I'll find some clothes, and you should take a shower. Then you can tell me what happened to your ear."

While the three of them fumbled with their shoes in the small entryway, trying to take them off without scattering the mud and pebbles stuck to the soles, Jim disappeared, his voice trailing off.

"You're lucky I'm on the night shift this week, so you found me at home. Otherwise, I'd be in the Lab during the day next week."

He reappeared with white t-shirts bearing the Lab's logo and some pants. "This is all I can offer. The pants might be too short for the guy, but you can roll them up to make them like shorts."

"Do you store work clothes here?" Judith asked, inspecting the clothes he handed out.

"You know I used to work in the office. I kept a few things; they come in handy sometimes!" Jim laughed.

By the time everyone had showered, Jim had prepared a little breakfast for them. The girl yawned as she ate; they were all exhausted. Tim looked ridiculous in the tight white t-shirt and pants that only reached mid-calf. As Jim had suggested earlier, he started rolling them up to knee length as if they were shorts.

"I can see you're tired, but I can only offer you a place to sleep on the floor. But first, tell me what brought you here and who your friends are," Jim inquired.

Judith squirmed uncomfortably. "Tim is my partner. We were retrieving something for Zack when I injured my ear."

Jim glanced at the black briefcase and then at Judith's ear. "Ah, right. I have some disinfectant here; let me get it!" He put down the toast he had just started eating.

He returned with a small bottle, pouring some blue liquid onto a cotton pad. Standing behind Judith, he began cleaning her ear, making her wince.

"Looks like a big chunk is missing. It would be better to bandage it. Was it shot off or what?"

"Yeah, it was," Judith replied, patiently holding her head still. Jim finished cleaning and went out to get a bandage. "I only have this, but we can cut it to size." He measured the gauze strip.

"The girl," Judith continued while waiting for Jim to bandage her ear, "is the tricky part. That's why we're here. She needs papers to get out of here."

Jim's hand froze mid-air, and then, holding the scissors and gauze, he sat on his chair. He stared at the child and then back at Judith. "Is this the kid everyone's looking for right now?"

This is it, thought Tim, quickly finishing the rest of his toast before they got kicked out.

"I'm afraid she is..." Judith began, but Jim, visibly agitated, threw everything from his hands onto the table, landing on his half-eaten toast.

"Seriously, you brought her here? Do you realize how much trouble you've caused? Of course you do!" he snapped, standing up and pacing repeatedly, running his hands through his hair.

"No one knows we're here... And Jim! You owe me! Have you forgotten what I did for you?"

"I know very well, but you can't keep bringing that up!"

"Just this once, and I'll never ask you for anything again!" Judith promised.

"You're out of your mind! You just said you got something back for Zack! Do you know that Zack is looking for this girl? And none other than Dash and his gang are looking for her!"

"They'll kill her if they find her! She's just a child! Do you want that, Jim? Are we going to take revenge on a kid?" Judith followed Jim with her eyes as he paced around the small room.

"If this gets out, I'm done for! Even just for taking you in! I should be sleeping now, you know? I'm on the night shift... I need to rest a bit till the evening!"

"Jim! Stop already! I don't want to blackmail you. I hate saying this, but if you don't help..." Judith left the sentence unfinished.

Jim walked over to a cupboard, took out a bottle, unscrewed the cap, and took a drink straight from it. He sighed deeply, took another sip, returned to his seat, and scrutinized the girl.

"How the hell did you get mixed up in this? Do you even know what you've gotten yourself into?" Jim worried.

Tim felt the need to interject: "It was an accident, really..." he said, immediately seeing the disdain in Judith's eyes. But she didn't want to rekindle their argument, so she didn't press the matter of fate versus accident.

"I know nothing about the situation, not even who she is. But that's not the point—she's just a child!" Judith defended herself. "And maybe it would be better if she got some sleep..."

Jim didn't move, though it was clear Judith didn't want to discuss things in front of the child.

"And now you've dragged me into this as if you can get away with anything!" Jim's voice revealed that he was starting to give in.

"All I'm asking is to send her away. I know you can arrange that. No one will ever find out!" Judith insisted.

Tim could already see from their newfound friend's demeanor that he couldn't resist further; Judith's arguments were compelling enough to convince him.

"So, you've already planned where you want to send her? Are you two going with her?" Jim inquired.

"We must deliver the briefcase to Zack; we're already late for the handover. We need to send her to Walnut Grove, to Noir."

"Uh-huh, so you'll notify Noir that you're sending someone? When does the portal open there?"

"It's open from nine to eleven. We need to send her over before that so no one sees."

"Okay, what's the time difference?" Jim asked though it seemed like he was mulling it over to himself. He moved to his desk, shuffling papers until he found what he sought. "Got it! Five hours. So, we need to have everything done within two hours."

"I need to notify Noir too. Do you still have the old fax machine?" Judith asked.

"Alright, if we've planned everything, let's get going. Has everyone finished breakfast?" Jim looked at the girl and Tim.

Tim nodded, and they all stood up. He thought they'd go through a side entrance into the Lab, but they didn't even need to leave the house.

The cupboard from which Jim had just taken the alcohol also functioned as a passageway. He opened both doors and by sliding the back panel, a tunnel opened up before them.

"Follow me, and stay quiet!" Jim took a lamp from the table and set off, followed by Judith, the girl, and Tim.

Tim couldn't see anything ahead of them, just the dimly lit figures before him. They walked for a long time, primarily straight, until it seemed they were heading upward.

The girl, whose name they still hadn't learned, moved deftly, not flinching even when they suddenly heard a rumbling noise. She held onto Judith's outstretched hand. This image stuck with Tim, seeing them move ahead in the flickering light, bound by an invisible bond. Judith, the savior. And for the first time, Tim wondered if Judith was right about fate. Two stray bullets and a piece of trash discarded in that exact spot had led this child to be walking ahead of him now. The thought sent a shiver down his spine.

This chain of events could trigger something in Judith that would also lead her to help Mara and forgive him for what he had done. Who knows? He just needed to broach the topic carefully, sensing that he sometimes needed help understanding his boss's thought process and conclusions.

Finally, those before him stopped, and they all entered a size-able office-like room. Desks were lined up in the center, and identical white cupboards lined the walls. They veered to the right into a smaller room that Jim unlocked. The windowless room was as white as the large one, with a desk, a camera, a photocopier, a scanner, and a cabinet. The four barely fit inside, but Jim locked the door behind them anyway.

"There's the fax machine. Try to contact Noir while I handle the paperwork," Jimmy instructed. What should the girl's name be?"

"We don't even know her real name," Tim replied.

Judith placed a piece of paper in front of the girl and handed her a pen to write her name. Tim couldn't see what she wrote, but Judith's reaction was enough to indicate something was wrong. As soon as the girl finished writing and Judith took the paper to read it, her mouth fell open.

"If you're going to tell me you didn't know..." Jimmy marveled. "You didn't know, did you? Do you see why I was so hesitant now?"

"Okay, I suspected I'd be in trouble, but I didn't know it would be this bad. Alright, the girl's name will be Elizabeth Toscano."

"Toscano, as in you'll be her mother?" Jimmy frowned.

"Yes, she'll be my hidden daughter. It's the best way I can protect her..."

"You will be Elizabeth from now on! Do you like this name?" asked Judith, the girl who found it pleasant, so she nodded. Then Judith tore the paper into tiny pieces, walked to the old-fashioned fax machine, and picked up the receiver.

Tim had never seen such a device and guessed it was there to avoid being eavesdropped on. Judith patiently waited for Noir to answer while Jimmy photographed the girl. He adjusted her blondish-brown hair, which was messy, with strands sticking out of the ponytail.

First, he untied the ponytail and, lacking a comb, smoothed it with his hands. Then he tried to get the girl to smile a little.

Tim felt useless and wondered if his boss would ever tell him who the girl's parents were.

Jimmy was already sitting at the computer, deeply engrossed in filling out the data. Judith was becoming impatient.

"Noir should be home in the morning, right? It should be around seven o'clock there, right?" she looked at Tim as if expecting help from him.

"He's usually home in the morning. Whenever I leave, he's always sitting outside his house. Moreover, he has others staying with him now. But does he have this fax machine at his house?" Tim began to worry about how they would reach Noir.

"Yes, he does. I'll write him a message, hoping he'll notice. I'll try Sara."

"Sara?" Tim was surprised.

"Yeah, you don't know much about them... but it's better this way."

Tim remembered Sara and how she knew about visiting Mara's lodging. He knew he couldn't trust her and felt an even greater urgency to tell his boss everything.

Judith suddenly sighed deeply. "Sara, listen to me. There's no time to explain! Please find Noir and tell him to check my message and call me back! Sara, it's essential. Hurry!"

Jimmy was already laminating the ID card and looked at the result satisfactorily. "I think it's better than the original."

They counted the minutes nervously as they waited for Noir to call them. "How long does it take for Sara to walk to Noir's place? Fifteen minutes?" Judith fretted.

"It might take Sara a bit longer..." Tim replied, picturing older people and overweight women hurrying along.

"We need to involve Sara more because I forgot inspectors were staying with Noir," Judith worried. It was almost eight o'clock their time when the fax rang loudly.

"Noir, finally!" Judith breathed a sigh of relief. "I'm sending a child over. I'll be there tomorrow; can you hide her until then? I was thinking of Sara... Yes, that'll work... Listen, how long will it take for you to get to the teleporter and start it up? Ten minutes? Great. We'll send her in ten minutes!"

They walked down more corridors until they reached a room where a Walnut Grove teleporter's replica stood in the middle, but this one was indoors. Jimmy activated it, and as its bluish light glowed, it returned old memories for Tim.

Judith knelt in front of the girl and calmly explained what would happen. She reassured her that she could trust Noir and Sara and that she would be there tomorrow.

"It's open," Jimmy alerted. "She can go now."

Judith accompanied the girl to the teleporter and waved her off. The girl stepped into the swirling blue vortex and disappeared suddenly as the teleporter quieted down.

CHAPTER 13

On the way back, Judith was driving and clearly in a much better mood. She rolled down the car window and enjoyed the wind blowing against her face. Jimmy had put a nice little bandage on her ear before they left.

Tim had never seen his boss in such high spirits while full of doubts. For instance, how would they explain the delay in delivering the prototype, or why were they wearing the lab shirts?

"I'm hungry! Shall we eat at that weird restaurant with only one hamburger?" Judith asked suddenly.

"We're already late, but that's fine. Let's have an omelet..." Tim replied with a slight pout.

"Oh, come on, Tim! Be a little happy! We did it. We saved the kid; she's in a safe place now. We have the prototype and need to deliver it to Zack. And then I'm done with all this..."

"Done? What do you mean?" Tim was surprised.

"I'm thinking of quitting. You think it was just a series of coincidences that led us to the girl, but I believe it was a sign. I no longer think this is my path. I need to do something else, and I see that now," she said firmly.

"Listen," Tim started hesitantly, feeling now that it was time for the confession. "I've been thinking about those who crossed over illegally and how to find them here. You probably know since you have connections."

Judith's expression turned serious. "What are you getting at? I'm not following."

"I mean that girl, Mara, who wanted to cross through me. We talked about how she might have crossed at another gate, and you said if she did, they'd hunt her down. But if they haven't found her, could you know where to look?" Tim was still probing, not wanting to reveal everything just yet.

"Mara? But what's with this girl? You're not worried about her, are you?" Judith smiled. "When we checked the system, we didn't find any record of her crossing anywhere else..."

"And what if she crossed at a gate where the gatekeeper erased her name from the system? And she's here. Where would you look?"

"Well, that's a good question. Mara might need to use her real name or have crossed under a different name. I'd look among the resistors hiding, but it could be better. Because if you look around, this island is a tourist paradise. The tourists are very well-documented, and they're very protected to ensure their peace isn't disturbed. The authorities are everywhere; even if they don't know each other personally, they all have IDs. The inspectors specialize in looking for illegal crossers. Then there's the support staff. They're also checked, but I'd look among them too."

"And do you think the inspectors will kill them if caught?" Tim asked worriedly.

"Why sugarcoat it? Yes, they likely will be killed after they extract all the information about their connections and how they crossed over... but what's with this girl? Are you worried she might have crossed over after all?"

"Yes," Tim admitted.

"You only met her once, and she had such an impact on you?"

"I can't explain it, but I fell for her. The way she looked at me... I can't get her out of my head."

"Well, Tim, I never thought you were such a romantic type! But be careful because the way she looked at you might have been to seduce you, to do everything she could to get you to let her through..."

"So, you also think I'm not good-looking enough for girls to notice me just for myself?"

This assumption took Judith aback.

"Understand me, please. You're a good-looking guy; it's not about that. It's about the circumstances. Think about it. A girl wants to cross the gate, and there's a gatekeeper. What means does the girl have to get through, especially if what she's doing isn't exactly legal? Wouldn't she use her charm? Maybe she did like you, but you also have to consider if her smile was for you specifically or if she would have smiled at anyone standing there to get across..."

Tim often lost in these thoughts, especially when his mood was low. He couldn't help but wonder if it was all just his imagination. That's why he yearned so much to meet the girl again, to confirm the reality of his feelings.

"Maybe that's exactly what I want—to find out what happened and see with my own eyes if her smile was meant for me."

"And you think she managed to cross over somehow? You can only find that out if you join the inspectors and search for the fugitives with them. Maybe they already know if she crossed over."

Finally, a glimmer of hope followed. Tim was happy and started feeling cheerful. He was no longer cold; they could feel they were nearing the coast because the air was much warmer and the vegetation was changing. Sometimes, palm trees towered above them, alternating with olive trees and colorful oleanders.

"If we're talking about destiny, maybe my destiny is to find and save that girl," Tim continued, his voice filled with a newfound hope.

"But wait, Tim! Don't forget that the girl is your enemy, and they are trying to get the invention at all costs—the one we're delivering back to Zack! They're working to destroy the system we live in!" Judith's objection was clear and firm, underscoring the tension between them.

"But now you want to quit, so I don't understand you again."

"Look, it's not that I'm questioning the authorities' work; I just don't see myself in it anymore. My role is over. I almost died, and it's time to turn my back on all this because I don't want to tempt fate."

Tim understood, yet needed to grasp the reasoning fully. "You've probably been on many missions; you've never gotten into a firefight?"

"I've been in interesting situations, but I've never been this close to death. And it made me think about what I want from life, what else is there for me, what else I need to do."

"Yes, the girl. Are you going to raise her?"

"As strange as it sounds, yes. I've always regretted not having children...."

Before they reached the small fishing village, they stopped at a gas station where they wanted to buy some shirts to change out of their own. Searching through the aisles, they couldn't find anything suitable. Judith was annoyed because they couldn't go to Zack in lab shirts, which would raise questions she didn't want to answer. She didn't want to stop at the same gas station either because it might make the clerk suspicious, and who knows whom they might tell...

They would have to stop by their lodging to change their outfits, which would take longer. But Judith was hungry and insisted on going to the restaurant.

As they approached the restaurant, they observed a picture of a girl on the door with the word "missing," along with a reward and a phone number. Judith's hand paused in mid-air as she opened the entrance door. They barely recognized the girl in the photo because, first of all, it was a school portrait, and secondly, she was posing with a broad smile. The girl they knew was a timid, sad child. The paper listed the girl's full name, and Tim realized the resistance leader was the man who was sentenced that day.

Inside the restaurant, they have seen the same picture. Maria's broad smile, the knitting lady, the man reading, and a few others were having coffee at the counter. Judith sat in the same spot again. Tim couldn't help but voice his discomfort about the place, surprised that Judith didn't remember the suited men from last time. "Doesn't that couple seem suspicious to you?" he asked, pointing to the knitting lady. "They look like they might be some kind of observers."

Judith took a closer look around. "We'll eat and be out of here. Their hamburger was divine last time... maybe you'll have one this time."

Maria flitted to them, and Tim wondered how she could creep that you wouldn't notice her approaching. Was it because of her shoes?

"Welcome back! What can I get you?" Maria smiled as she poured them coffee.

Both knew there was no point in looking at the menu, although Tim was doing just that.

"Did you get a delivery, and can Tim finally taste your delicious hamburger?" Judith asked hopefully.

"Yes, just this morning. If you want a hamburger, you might have to wait a bit for the patties to defrost."

To Tim's surprise, Judith nodded, agreeing to wait. The waitress disappeared, and Tim's feeling that something was off grew stronger. Judith, however, was unreasonably cheerful.

"This might be our last meal together!" she leaned closer to Tim. We'll take the briefcase to Zack, and if you're still set on that crazy idea of finding Mara, I can recommend you to Zack. After all, you know what she looks like, which might make it easier to see her. Forget her name; it's probably fake anyway."

"And you're leaving." Tim agreed.

"But you know you can't tell anyone about what happened. Besides, you're in this up to your neck, too."

Tim nodded, starting to understand this world better. "I'm going to the restroom," he said hastily. The restroom was next to the kitchen, and he could hear someone arguing loudly, though he couldn't make out the words. The restroom itself had surprisingly improved since their last visit. Small soaps of various scents were placed in funny little holders. He didn't quite understand the need for so many, but he appreciated the thoughtfulness of choosing a soap that appealed to him. There was also liquid soap with a dispenser, so the small soaps were puzzling.

He sniffed each of them. Then, as he exited the restroom, he almost bumped into the chef, Peter, whom he had seen on their previous visit. However, he had a strange feeling that he had seen this man before. Then it hit him—the same Peter who had approached him, referring to Mara, trying to get him to let him through. At that time, Peter was wearing a hood, so Tim could barely see his face, so he only now recognized him in the dimly lit hallway. The chef was surprised but said nothing, quickly disappearing into the kitchen.

When he sat down with Judith, he needed to tell her about the incident. "This will sound strange, but maybe we should leave... listen, the chef, Peter. I've seen him back home. After Mara tried to get through to me, Peter also contacted me."

"Are you sure it was him?"

"Yeah, but the inspectors had taken him out of the line. So, I need to understand how he managed to get here.

"Ohh, the problem is bigger; there's a gate where they can easily get through. We need to report this, let's go." She grabbed the black briefcase, and they stood up. The door opened, and Dash walked in with his four companions.

Seeing them, Judith decided to sit back down. "This is just what we needed!" she whispered, pulling Tim down by the arm, who still wanted to leave.

"What a pleasant surprise!" Dash approached them, pushing his sunglasses up onto his head. His companions sat at the nearby free table, boredly flipping through the menu. Dash pulled out a chair and sat next to Judith.

"Hope you found the girl!" Judith tried to sound pleasant.

Dash squinted his blue eyes and smiled, showing all 32 teeth. "Do you think if we had found her, her picture would be plastered all over town?"

Judith pretended as if she had just realized the girl on the posters was the same. "We had quite a busy night; I didn't pay attention to the papers..."

"Even though it's impossible, I couldn't help but think you might know more about the girl. Oddly, you were right there, and then the girl just disappeared."

"Coincidences happen more often than you'd think!" Judith smiled.

Maria appeared with two hamburgers and placed them before Tim and Judith. Tim looked at the vast bun, slightly toasted with sesame seeds on top, in satisfaction. It smelled incredibly enticing, and the fries were just how he liked them. He didn't care about anything else, only that he could take a bite.

Dash and Judith watched in astonishment as he devoured the food. "Like I said, we had a pretty busy day; we didn't even have time to eat," Judith apologized, reaching for her fries.

Maria reappeared and poured coffee for the new arrivals. "I'll try the hamburger too; it looks delicious," Dash ordered, then continued the previous conversation. "I've decided not to believe you. And since you're suspicious, it's best to take the briefcase, whatever is in it, and deliver it to Zack myself."

Judith swallowed the fry in her mouth. "The briefcase is none of your business; it's my assignment, and I will deliver it!"

"I don't know who you are, but you should know I'm in charge here. If I say I'm taking the briefcase, that's how it will be!" Dash smiled again, his voice measured and calm, not wanting to draw attention.

"As you said, you have no idea who I am. So you'd better watch your words." Judith replied, also in a calm tone, as if they were chatting about the weather. Meanwhile, Tim had already stuffed the last bites into his mouth and brought the fries closer to himself. But he couldn't start tasting them because Dash pulled out a gun and pointed it at Judith.

Judith, however, also drew a gun and aimed it at Dash. A bit delayed, Tim stood up and aimed at the four suited men, who pointed their weapons at them.

This standoff was disrupted when suddenly all the seemingly random customers pulled out guns, aiming at Dash's group and Judith's. Even the two old folks and Maria had weapons in their hands.

Chapter 14

Time seemed to stand still in the restaurant as everyone froze, holding their breath. The murderous midday sun filtered through the window, which faced west. No one had had the time to lower the blinds, and the sunlight crept further into the room, casting larger and larger patches of light across the tabletops. The silence was so profound that they could hear the sizzling of meat from the kitchen. The chef and the kitchen helper, both holding guns, stood with the others, and no one paid attention to the food anymore. The smell of burnt meat and scorched onions would fill the air in a few minutes.

There was also another smell already noticeable. The chef, Peter, had been boiling milk, as he always had coffee with milk after lunch. He had forgotten to remove it from the stove in the rush of events. He knew that once the milk boiled, it would spill over the pot and burn onto the electric stove. The smell of burnt milk was the first sign that the kitchen was unattended.

Judith stood opposite the kitchen, locking eyes with Dash, who stood with his back to the people at the counter, unaware of the three men aiming their guns at them. He could see the two old folks at the table near the entrance, Maria, and two more people from the kitchen, all poised for action.

Only Tim, oblivious to the armed people behind him, faced Judith, his gun aimed at Dash's men. Judith, quick to assess the situation, hissed to Tim without moving, her voice trembling with fear: "Maria!"

Tim, in a state of confusion, obeyed and turned his gun towards the waitress. This sudden shift caused a wave of uncertainty as everyone scrambled to find a more advantageous position in the chaotic scenario.

The four men in suits had their guns trained on Judith and Tim. They had yet to realize whose side the random-seeming patrons were on. Judith, however, began to suspect, based on what Tim had said about the chef, that this place might be filled with resistance members. This meant she should theoretically be allied with Dash, but she saw no hope of that at the moment.

Judith and Tim appeared to be at a disadvantage if panic broke out, but by directing Tim to Maria, Judith hoped to buy some time.

Everyone was waiting for some signal. Tim awaited Judith's, Dash's men awaited his, and the others awaited Maria's. Judith quickly noticed this. She saw the older man sitting by the bookshelf rise slowly, trying to position himself before Maria. She didn't like that move.

"Hey! Stop! No tricks!" Judith shouted. Meanwhile, Dash stared in bewilderment at those standing behind him, perhaps just then assessing the situation himself.

The smell from the kitchen became increasingly unpleasant.

Dash felt the need to clarify the situation, sensing a complete misunderstanding. "I think everyone should calm down!" Judith didn't understand what he expected—everyone would put away their guns and sit nicely?

No one moved, so Dash continued. "We just want to deal with these two here. You do not need to get involved... I'll tell you what. We'll leave the restaurant and won't bother you any longer. Is that okay?"

Still, no one moved, so Dash felt compelled to explain further. "Look, you've all seen the girl's picture all over town. We're looking for her; I believe these two know where she is. I think you know who the girl is, and it wouldn't be good for you to cross me or hinder the authorities' work."

Tim sensed that Dash adopted an official tone to bolster his point and emphasize his authority.

The older woman then did something unexpected—she spat. No one anticipated that. Judith realized that Dash still had no clue where they were or who the others were. But Maria's deep, commanding voice quickly clarified things for him. "If you think your white-collar talk will get you anywhere here, you're sorely mistaken! We don't care!" The older woman spat on the floor again, a clear sign of their defiance.

Dash became more cautious, and Judith could see sweat beading on his temple, with one drop starting to slide down. Finally, he gets it, she thought.

"I'll tell you what," Dash tried again. "Everyone lowers their weapons, and we'll leave quietly. No one will ever know we were here. We'll stay far away from you. Though I'm sorry I couldn't try your hamburger, but from the smell, I guess I won't..."

The smell of smoke was already spreading from the kitchen, and it was only a matter of time before it became visible.

The three men at the counter looked expectantly at Maria. She said nothing, just stared at them intently, especially at Tim, as he was the only one aiming at her.

"For heaven's sake, how long will we stand here like this?" Dash grew impatient. "We just came here for lunch, and we're looking for that kid, which is pretty crucial. A child alone out in the scorching sun! Have you thought about that?"

"You forgot to mention how that child got lost!" Judith hissed.

"I knew it!" Dash furrowed his brow. "I knew you were involved. Did you spy on us? And then hide her in the car? Is that what happened?"

Judith realized she had made a big mistake. "You're imagining things. I'm just deducing who the girl is. Whose idea was it to write her name on the paper?"

More beads of sweat appeared on Dash's forehead, and it was hard to tell whether it was from the scorching sun, which now fully illuminated the tables, or the tense situation.

"What is your name?" Maria finally spoke, now aiming her pistol decisively at Dash.

"Me? Dash..." he replied, somewhat relieved that communication had finally started.

"Dash, listen up. Only I can decide what happens here. You are all in my house! And you may not know it yet, but you've come to a very wrong place. I'm surprised you, super law enforcement people, have yet to figure out who we are. Or where you are. So it's getting annoying that you keep coming here and causing trouble. At least once a day, I have to kick out some armed thug who thinks they have more rights than us just because they have a gun and a badge. Well, enough is enough! And believe me, if I could, I'd put up a sign saying no entry for law enforcement, but unfortunately, that would make us your target.

Dash blinked several times, trying to piece together what he had heard. Judith leaned in a bit to help: "FYI."

"Thank you, dear!" Maria laughed. "I immediately saw that you two are smarter, though the fact you returned doesn't fit the picture. My chef told me interesting things about the high-ups, Tim, right?"

Tim felt faint. He feared his boss would find out what he had done under similar circumstances. He should have told her the thing with Mara already.

"But you're not the main targets, though I'm curious about what's in that black briefcase... But first, you five. That kid is just a kid; why are you looking for her? What's the order if you find her? I have a guess, so I hope you never do!"

"Do you know something? Hm? Out with it! It obstructs justice if you don't tell us what you know!" Dash blurted out.

"Even if we knew something, we wouldn't tell you. You can be sure we'll do everything to keep her out of your hands!" Maria concluded, but Dash didn't let it go.

"I don't understand what's going on here. What is this all about? If we start shooting here, do you think anyone will survive?"

Tim had to admit that Dash was right. If they started shooting, he, Judith, and Dash would be the primary targets because they were in the worst position in the middle. One of Dash's men and Maria might survive. Perhaps even the chef if he quickly ran into the kitchen.

These thoughts crossed his mind, and he wondered if Peter might know where Mara was. But the tension was palpably rising, and everyone was watching each other's movements.

"You're right; we'd probably shoot everyone, especially you." Maria grinned, showing none of her friendly demeanor when pouring coffee earlier.

"Then I suggest we find out what's in the briefcase. I understand it's going to Zack." With this comment, Dash hit the mark, and Judith realized he had cleverly deflected attention from himself.

"Let me tell you what's going to happen now," Judith began very seriously, determinedly. "Under no circumstances will I open this briefcase. And I'll tell you why. I almost died twice because of it. You see the bandage on my ear? That's from a stray bullet. And before that, it was a jammed gun that saved my life. I've never noticed signs or fate, thinking the universe is trying to tell me something. Have you ever paid attention to signs? Right now, I see that all of us standing here are not in an accident. There's a reason for everything; fate brought us here to this place at this moment." As Judith spoke, she gestured with her free hand but kept her aim on Dash with the other.

"Today, I was about to have my last meal with Tim, my partner, because I'm leaving. That's right, I've had enough because you know what? Until today, I thought I controlled everything and did whatever I wanted. But those two stray bullets made me think about fate and about how I don't want to kill anyone anymore. Do you understand? No one! So, let's ask the question: if all hell breaks loose here, who might survive? Dash? Do you think you'll survive? We're standing right in the middle. But you've already thought this through, so you're sweating like this. Maria? Do you think you'll survive? Tim's aiming at you, and believe me, the kid's a damn good shot, and even if the older man is ready to jump, you can be sure the four well-dressed guys behind me are aiming at you. So what do we gain from all this?"

Judith paused, and Tim thought for the first time that Judith wouldn't shoot. What would happen to them, or was she planning this crazy talk her way out of it?

"Look, I mean it when I say we're not here by accident, and this not-by-accident happened so you could meet me here, so I could tell you how valuable you all are. Every one of you. Who wants to die just like that? And you know, as well as I do, that this madness can only end one way: with everyone here getting riddled with bullets. Unless you listen to reason, and we all walk out of here. Tim and I will take this briefcase to its owner. Dash will keep looking for the kid, and you can check the kitchen because, judging by the smoke, everything's on fire."

Judith paused again. The older man in front of the bookshelf hesitantly lowered his arm, and it wasn't clear if it was because Judith's words moved him or because his arm was tired. Since he only dropped it briefly, it was probably the latter, but Maria seemed affected by Judith's speech.

"There is some truth in what you say. Obviously, no one wants to die willingly, and this situation is quite the stalemate; very likely, we'd all kill each other," Maria said.

"Dash, what do you think?" Judith asked.

"There's something to it, but our matter isn't resolved..."

"Oh, come on! Everyone has their own business! I have a job to do, you have a job to do, and so do Maria and her people. Let's leave these petty grievances behind!"

Dash nodded.

"So, I'll tell you what happens next! This sentence has been said a lot today..." Judith tried to joke, but everyone felt they wanted to move on. "Dash, and you four, you leave first. And I suggest you don't wait for us around the corner because someone might find out you're trying to cross us."

Judith motioned for them to leave. With their guns half-lowered, they headed for the door. Once they stepped outside, those inside followed them with their eyes as they got into their car and drove off.

"Now it's our turn," Judith started. "I think we should put away the guns. Hm?" she asked, looking at Maria.

Maria nodded, and everyone breathed a little easier. The chef and the kitchen maid went back into the kitchen.

"I'm taking the hamburger with me, though I'm a bit sorry it's gone cold." And they headed out. Tim took a deep breath as they got outside, not believing they might get out of this whole adventure unscathed.

CHAPTER 15

J udith and Tim were on their way to Zack, and Judith was busy eating her hamburger in the car, paying attention to things not falling. She failed, as her lab T-shirt was already messy, and pieces of onion fell into her lap.

Tim watched patiently at first, then decided they needed to stop somewhere. He pulled off the road, and Judith got out to finish the last bites. She was satisfied with herself, as she hadn't wasted the hamburger, and they had survived the day.

Tim waited for further instructions, wondering whether they should return to their accommodation or go straight to Zack. Judith wiped her face and hands, rinsed her mouth with water, and roughly cleaned her clothes. She got back into the car and gave the order to start.

"To Zack?" Tim asked.

"Yes, we're not that far away. Let's get rid of this damn briefcase!"

Tim didn't argue; it was his fondest wish, too. "What do you think about Dash? Won't he get in our way?"

Judith seemed to ponder. "Possibly. Do you think he has it in him to cross us? Now that I think about it, he might. He lost a child and wants to score points with Zack... How good are you at hiking?"

Tim feared Judith knew a shorter route, though he didn't think it would be without the car. They didn't even return to their accommodation, which would have been foolish as it might have been found by now. They headed towards the mountains and unexpectedly drove into the forest. Unexpectedly, because nothing indicated there was a road there. At Judith's direction, Tim drove further among the trees so their car wouldn't be visible from the road.

"Walking, then? I've always dreamed of this... ever since I've been with you, I'm constantly climbing mountains or swimming..." Tim said.

"At least you're not bored... What do you think? Is it better than standing by the boring teleport gate at home?"

"Well, it was a bit more predictable..."

"Come on, don't whine, you wanted to come along! Remember?"

The forest was cool and quiet. They walked in silence, side by side, still affected by the events of the past hours, especially Tim. He thought about how little he still understood about this world.

"There are so many things I don't understand. Can I ask? For example, why did the authorities not know about that restaurant? I thought we had everything under control."

Judith looked at Tim worriedly. "I told you about the service staff, that they're also monitored—every employee. But there's a flaw in the system, and a big one if we missed this. Somehow, they're in the system as reliable workers... And that Maria, what a character she was!" she recalled.

This statement surprised Tim. Why was she jumping between thoughts? "So there's a gate where they pass through as reliable staff?"

"Probably. And if Peter, the chef who was even pulled out of line for you, still managed to get through, it means there's a suspicious inspector in Walnut Grove, too. I'll have to look into that tomorrow."

Tim felt this was the moment to confess everything. "There's something I should have told you a long time ago. And believe me, I've tried and started to tell you several times, but I was always afraid that if I told you, I'd bring trouble on myself and Mara."

"Mara? That girl again..."

"I let Mara through..." Tim yelled out, bracing himself for anything—Judith might yell or shoot him on the spot.

Judith stopped and looked at him questioningly. "You let her through? How?"

"Do you remember when you gave me the list and the codes? The erase code. Well, I erased Mara from the system, too..." Tim awaited her reaction, but Judith just kept walking.

"So the girl batted her eyelashes, you let her through, and then erased her as if nothing happened..."

"Yes, but I know it was terrible of me, and that's why I'm here, why I wanted to come over—to make up for my mistake, to find the girl and bring her back."

At this point, Judith stopped and turned to face Tim. "If I told you to find her and kill her, would you do it?"

Tim just stood there, realizing he should have considered this possibility too.

"So you wouldn't. And if I told you to find Mara and let someone else kill her?"

Tim stared at Judith with the same dismal expression as before.

"Then what do you want, Tim? Or what do you expect? What do you want from me? To pat you on the back and praise you? Now I understand why you asked those strange questions..."

Tim struggled to respond, as this was different from his expected reaction. "What if I just found her and brought her back?"

"Just that?" Judith said incredulously. "Do you think it works like that?"

"And what about fate? I came with you because of Mara. My goal has always been to find her and see her again. What would have happened if I wasn't with you?" he hinted, not mentioning the two stray bullets.

"I thought you wanted to become an inspector because you were tired of the gatekeeper job... and you even got a commendation for not letting anyone through..." She recalled, slapping her forehead. She started walking again through the forest, and Tim followed.

His boss didn't want to discuss the incident anymore, but Tim needed to know what she thought. As they walked, weaving between the trees, he kept glancing at her face, trying to read her expression. But Judith just kept walking, and her face mostly showed contempt. Tim didn't want to say goodbye to Judith like this because he was determined to stay and find the girl at any cost.

"If you don't help me, I'll find her myself!" Tim finally said.

Judith stopped again. "You're crazy! And we've already talked about how the girl just used you. Was there something between you? Is that why you let her through?"

"What? No, nothing..."

"So you're saying she smiled at you, and that was enough? Or did she convince you of the resistance's doctrines? Are you one of them? Do you believe in them?"

"No, not at all... she didn't recruit me, relax!"

"And did you let Peter through, too?"

"No! I swear, only Mara. No one else!"

Judith looked into Tim's eyes for a long time as if trying to read the truth from them. The boy held her gaze; he had nothing else to hide.

"So you want to find her and take her away from here? Even if it turns out I was right, and her smile was random, she would have flirted with anyone standing there?"

Tim took a deep breath, as he had no idea how he would find out. "I don't want her to get hurt here..."

"You are crazy.

With that, Judith declared the conversation over with her actions, stubbornly moving forward until they reached a valley. They saw a building that resembled a vacation home, and as they descended, Tim noticed cameras mounted on the fence, which seemed odd in this setting.

They reached a road, and after a short walk, they heard the sound of cars and then the screech of brakes. They were stopped, the inspectors asked for their details, and then they announced over the phone. Everything seemed fine as they were placed in one of the cars and driven to the fortress-like house. No one touched the black briefcase.

They entered a dining room-like area, and Tim was seated at the table. Judith continued into a smaller room where a stocky, bald man sat with his back to them, holding a smoking cigar while listening to Judith's report. Tim only caught fragments of the conversation.

A man armed at the wall stood like a statue. Tim whispered to him, asking for the restroom. The unfriendly guard pointed the way with an upraised hand, giving Tim a once-over. Still in his lab shirt, Tim looked into the mirror in the restroom and saw how messy he appeared. Sweat and dust had dried on his forehead, making him look like a child playing in a sandbox.

He washed his face and only noticed the small soap bars in the strange little kitschy holders. This was familiar, and it struck him that it might not be a coincidence that he had seen similar ones at the restaurant.

Returning to the long dining table, he found someone else sitting there: a lively-eyed, goat-bearded man in his forties. The man stared at Tim intensely, and Tim couldn't understand why he looked that way. What was wrong with him? Tim tried to stare back, but the man's piercing gaze was too much for him.

From somewhere, a butler-like figure appeared—at least Tim thought he was a butler because he brought a half-liter bottle of mineral water on a silver tray and a glass filled with ice and lemon slices, which he placed in front of the goat-bearded man.

Tim was astonished. He had been there first and was about to ask for a drink, too, but the butler didn't even glance at him. Instead, he bowed profoundly and entered Judith and Zack's room.

Tim heard Judith asking for water, and Zack raised his empty glass. Tim tried to catch the butler's eye, but he skillfully turned in the other direction, giving Tim no chance to speak.

Tim was annoyed. Why didn't Judith say anything on his behalf? The goat-bearded man noticed all of Tim's efforts, and instead of being considerate, he played up Tim's apparent thirst. The man theatrically poured himself a glass of water, drank it all, and then looked at Tim as he poured the rest of the water into his glass, not drinking it but just playing with the glass's foggy surface with his fingers.

Tim couldn't believe his eyes. He had never encountered such rudeness. What had he done to deserve this man's hostility?

He pondered this when Judith and Zack stood up, said their goodbyes, and even embraced each other for a while—Tim assumed she was telling Zack she was quitting. Then Judith came toward them, and when Zack noticed the goat-bearded man, he greeted him loudly: "Bernard!"

Tim whispered in surprise to Judith, "Is that Bernard, the inventor?"

Judith nodded and pulled Tim by the arm to introduce him to Zack. "This is the one I was talking about, Tim."

They shook hands, and Zack's firm grip took Tim aback. "Alright, Tim, Judith will tell you what you need to know, and I'll see you on Monday," Zack said, then turned towards the inventor, signaling that the conversation was over for him.

As they walked out, Tim watched Zack embrace the inventor like an old friend. Was he confused? Yes, because Tim knew Bernard had sold the prototype to the resistance. When they got into their car -God knew who brought it there—he asked Judith about it, and she started driving towards their accommodation.

"No, he didn't sell it; the FYI has stolen from him. And now they're negotiating for him to sell the teleportation plans to Zack. For a good price, of course..."

Tim waited for an explanation concerning his situation, watching Judith intently. "I know you're curious about what I arranged for you... Listen, I want to help. You have three days to find Mara and send her back, then on Monday, you'll come here; Zack has hired you as an insider. You'll carry out assignments. I told him how well you aim, so I've done everything to ensure you can stay here.

Regarding Mara, I can help by sending you to Lenny. He has access to all the employee databases; you can review them. I told him you're looking for a fugitive, which is true. But listen, you'll recognize her by her picture, but don't reveal her. If you identify her, remember her name and where she works, then move on. Pretend you didn't find her. That's all I can do for you."

"And you? What will happen to you?" Tim inquired.

"I told Zack about the two stray bullets; he understood and let me go. So, I'm heading to Jim's in the morning."

"If I find Mara, where can I send her back? Can I take her to Jim?"

Judith shook her head. "You still haven't given up on this madness, have you? Promise me you won't act like a lovesick puppy and try to stay grounded in reality. That girl probably wants the invention. Or now, they want the plans because the prototype is with Zack. Remember that this is likely her primary goal, whatever she does or says. I understand you feel something for her and don't want her to die. But promise me you won't go further than that. Don't help her acquire the invention, for instance."

Tim nodded in agreement.

"If you understand this and act accordingly, there won't be any trouble. I'll speak to Jim on your behalf. He won't be happy and will likely want to chase you away, but he's helpful. So, take her to Jim and send her back. If you go with her, be prepared to become a fugitive, and the authorities will hunt you down. Mara probably has contacts, and you'll be able to hide. You must decide if you want that kind of life. Or you'll build a career here as a top inspector on Zack's team."

CHAPTER 16

J udith quickly said her goodbyes, as she had no business there. Tim found himself back at their accommodation, realizing he should rest, but somehow, he couldn't. Holding the address where he was supposed to go the following day—to Lenny, about whom he knew nothing, he hesitated. What should he expect? Judith, who seemed to navigate on this island so well, had suddenly disappeared, leaving him still puzzled about many things.

He wondered if Peter at the restaurant would consider him an enemy. Could Peter help him locate Mara? He may not need to involve Lenny, an authority member, and could put Mara in danger if he realized who Tim was looking for. On the other hand, Peter might be more efficient in helping him. Tim needed to find out if he had Peter's trust, but being with Judith placed him in the opposing camp. It was worth probing into, but he needed more courage to return to the restaurant and risk fate. It was too risky.

So, he stuck to the original plan: rest now, then visit Lenny tomorrow. Sleep wouldn't come, though he felt tired and hungry. He sat up in bed and started walking somewhere, unsure where. His thoughts raced through his mind. He had three days to find

Mara—if that was even her real name—convince her, or rather, figure out what was between them and save her from here.

He walked toward the beach, realizing that apart from when they swam across, he had yet to go down to the shore. He had seen the soothing waves of the sea a few times from the car, but that was his only connection to it. Why was this so important? He didn't understand it, but the past day's events, the rush, always brought him back to one comforting image: seeing the sea from the car. The sight of the sea calmed him.

When he reached the beach, he felt the same calm. He watched the soothing waves and succumbed to their call. He left his sandals on the shore and walked into the water. The water was pleasantly warm; it didn't feel cold as the sun didn't warm up his body. He was almost alone on the beach, except for someone walking a dog and a couple sitting on the shore, embracing each other.

He swam pretty far into the sea until he could no longer hear his swirling thoughts, only feeling the pain in his arms and the ache in his breath. He was tired and not used to such prolonged swimming. He turned back towards the shore, and as he looked at the shore, he was struck by the stunning view. The blue-gray outlines of the mountain range behind the promenade, the deep blue sky filled with countless stars, and when he lay on his back, he saw the Milky Way above him. His ears were underwater, and he heard the sea's hum. He never wanted to forget this moment, no matter what happened in the coming days.

When he felt rested enough, he began swimming back to the shore. It was pleasant to reach the shore again; the person with the dog and the couple had disappeared, leaving him alone, panting as he searched for his sandals. He found them but didn't put them on, holding them in his hand as he walked barefoot back to his accommodation. As he walked, his clothes dripped with water, but he didn't care.

Tim had difficulty waking up the following day and left in a hurry, still sleepy. He headed to see Lenny, who worked in an office building. Tim thought there was probably no police force on the island, but this building reminded him of a government agency's headquarters. There was no sign indicating what the place was, but the grumpy face of the receptionist and the fact that they called to announce his arrival suggested it was indeed an official place. When he went up to the designated floor, a young man with blond hair appeared from behind one of the doors and waved at him.

"You're Tim, right? Judith has told me a lot about you, that you're looking for a woman who's a runaway and might be among the employees. Come on in!" He welcomed Tim warmly and led him into a small room, which he unlocked with a key. To Tim's surprise, he didn't have to stare at a computer screen; instead, he had to search through physical printed files from boxes. It felt like the Stone Age, Tim thought. On the floor were numerous boxes, dated and stacked in towers.

"Wow, are there this many?" Tim was horrified, not wanting to spend hours there. He realized he had overestimated the system.

"The problem is that we have the files of everyone who has ever worked here. The boxes are dated, and you're lucky you only need to check those without an end date, as I assume the woman you are looking for is still here."

Lenny's suggestion was a good lead, and he could also narrow down the starting date. So, he only had to go through three boxes. Lenny was very helpful in sorting out the women's files for Tim, so he only had to look through those.

"I hope I recognize her; I've only seen her once, but she was very suspicious," Tim explained. "I'll set aside those who resemble her even slightly."

"Should I sort them by hair color, too, perhaps?" Lenny offered.

"She might have dyed or cut her hair, which wouldn't help," Tim declined.

Tim felt Lenny wasn't watching his every move and seemed genuinely helpful. Perhaps Judith had overthought the situation, but Tim still took care not to raise any suspicion about Mara. He had already set aside five files in the "resembles her" pile, carefully choosing the least similar ones. He had gone through two boxes and worried she might not be in the last one either. Lenny neatly arranged the previous box of female employees, and few were left.

"Lenny, could I get a glass of water? I'm a bit thirsty," Tim asked.

"Of course, I'll get it right away. The dust can dry out your throat, and plenty of that here."

Tim quickly flipped through the remaining files, and as soon as Lenny left, the last one was Mara. Her hair was blonde in the picture, but he immediately recognized her by her kindly face. The name on the file was Patricia Lubica, and her workplace was a receptionist at the Hilton Hotel. This fact stunned Tim because the hotel was nearby; they passed it almost daily. If she worked there...

Lenny returned with the glass of water, and Tim pretended he hadn't finished yet, sighing more and more to let Lenny know that. "Unfortunately, I didn't see her among the files. Or maybe I didn't recognize her from the pictures."

"Maybe it would be worth checking the suspicious ones in person?" Lenny suggested, quickly gathering the files from the "suspicious" pile. He photocopied them and readily handed them to Tim. Tim thanked him for his kindness and felt very sorry for the five women he might have randomly put in jeopardy.

Tim didn't care if it looked suspicious to go straight to the hotel from Lenny's; he wanted to find out as quickly as possible if the file was accurate. Was she working as a receptionist? He showed his ID to the hotel doorman, who promptly opened the door for him.

Stepping into the hotel lobby felt like entering another world. The spaces were vast, with no ceiling in sight—well, there was one, but a transparent glass roof illuminated a sprawling tree in the center with natural light. Tim didn't recognize what kind of tree it was. Its gnarled brown branches ended in red leaves. It was beautiful, and he almost thought it wasn't real, but the fact that they had placed it under the glass roof to bask in the sunlight suggested it was a real tree. Around the tree were sofas and tables where guests chatted and enjoyed the pleasant environment. There was even a real piano with someone playing it. The walls and columns were decorated with stucco of all sorts of colorful shapes.

Tim felt dizzy from the luxury, but Mara was the only one who really captivated him. She stood at the counter, with no one in front of her, engrossed in something, looking down. Her blonde hair, tightly pinned back in a bun, looked strange but suited her.

Tim watched her, savoring the moment of finally seeing her and knowing she was okay. He didn't know his next move or words; his plan had only gone as far as finding her. Mara seemed to sense someone was staring at her from the entrance because she suddenly looked up directly at Tim. She was stunned.

Then she stepped back, opened a small door, and called someone because another woman in the same uniform appeared to take over at the counter. Mara walked toward Tim slowly and deliberately. When she almost reached him, she signaled for him to follow her, not through the main entrance but through a smaller door farther away.

It must have been a staff entrance because it opened to the side.

Tim was speechless as they stood facing each other. "So here you are, you found me..." Mara began uncertainly, and Tim realized she might think she was in trouble.

"Is Mara your real name?" was Tim's first question to her, then quickly added, "I'm not here as a gatekeeper. I want to help you because it's only a matter of time before they find you..."

The girl frowned, not entirely understanding the situation. "Ahh, so you want to help?"

"Yes, I want to make up for the mistake of letting you through. I want to take you back," Tim yelled out.

"You're confusing me. So, did the authorities send you? I don't understand..." The situation was confusing, and Tim realized he needed a more concrete reason.

"Look," Tim began, "I think I fell in love with you because I haven't been able to get you out of my head since we met. And I'm afraid you'll get into trouble here, so I came over to check if you're okay."

A weight lifted off Tim's chest. But the girl was puzzled.

"Wow! That's a bit intense! But you came because of me? And you're not working for the authorities?" Mara asked, and Tim could honestly deny working for Zack since his job there would start on Monday, two days from now.

"Because of you, and I'm not with the authorities."

"This is crazy... but Tim, remember? I have a mission here. I can only leave once it's done... I need to deliver the invention..."

Tim thought the resistance had insufficient information since the prototype was already with Zack, and Bernardt was also about to sell the documentation to Zack. "If you want, I can help..." Tim began, not entirely understanding himself. "But I'd need you to complete everything in two days. You can't be here by Monday..."

"Do you know something? What's happening on Monday?" Mara asked, concerned.

"I can't tell you, but promise you'll cross back with me on Sunday night." Tim was determined for the first time, and his hand caressed her face. He didn't know where he found the courage, but he traced her lips with his fingers. He had dreamed of this so much! Tim heard her say something but couldn't focus on the words. He was captivated by the shape of her mouth. When Mara instinctively wetted her lips, he couldn't resist any longer. He pulled her closer and kissed her. Mara was surprised but didn't resist. He was feeling her lips on his like magic.

Tim was over the moon with happiness. Mara began to plan, thinking she needed to introduce Tim to some resistance members because they knew where the documentation could be found. But for that, they needed to trust Tim.

"Tim, you might have to prove you genuinely want to help. I admit I'm still a bit uncertain... no one has ever done something this kind for me..."

Tim still had his arm around her waist and kissed her forehead. "I'll go with you anywhere, and I want to be with you constantly for these two days to ensure nothing happens to you."

Mara laughed. "It might be smarter if I introduce you as someone already on our side. You already know Peter..."

Tim's face darkened slightly. "Yes, Peter, he's the cook at that oddly named restaurant, something rooster..."

"Exactly, The Rooster. So, if we both stand up for you, the others will believe you're one of us." Mara smiled encouragingly.

"There was a bit of a scuffle at the Rooster yesterday... Dash was there with his gang. Peter might have misjudged the situation and might think I'm with the authorities... I just needed the information on where you were, so I contacted them. But I have nothing to do with them otherwise..."

"I heard about it. You were there?" Mara frowned. "Were you the one with the black briefcase?"

Tim suspected that this would be challenging. He wanted to convince Mara that he was on their side, which meant he was also starting a relationship with a lie. Was it a good idea? But maybe, once they got through this, Mara would understand that he did it for her good.

Tim nodded, trying to explain. "To find you, I had to do certain things. That was one of them. But didn't Peter tell you that it's thanks to us there wasn't a bullet storm?" He smiled reassuringly at Mara. She leaned in and kissed him, then pushed herself away.

"I need to get back to work now. I finish in the afternoon. Will you come for me? Then we can discuss everything."

They agreed, and Tim spent the rest of the day planning to prove to Peter that he was trustworthy.

CHaPTer 17

Tim discovered a new side of the place that he had never noticed. During the day, downtown's small, narrow streets were sleepy and empty, but people were bustling everywhere at night. Tourists spent their money in shops selling trinkets or eating local specialties in restaurants. Mara held his hand, trying to navigate through the leisurely strollers. She was in a hurry. There was a bar where they met the other resistance members on Friday night.

Tim found himself neck-deep in things, having integrated into the FYI organization so quickly that he could hardly keep up. At this point, he had no specific goal, only one thing on his mind: Mara. Whatever was happening around them was just a side concern. The fact that he had been introduced to Zack yesterday and would now have a beer with the FYI organization did not bother him morally. Not at this point.

Mara's scent and proximity enchanted him, and he couldn't take his eyes off her. It was as if he were bewitched, behaving like someone who only thought one step ahead. This behavior was not typical of Tim. Having meticulously planned how to come over for Mara, he had lost all judgment. He marveled at everything like a child. The fact that they didn't sit among the guests when entering the small bar but instead headed down to the basement through a dark corner didn't even register with him because Mara was holding his hand, and he was watching her loose hair playfully sway.

He lost his sense of reason, and perhaps this naivety saved him. Because as soon as they reached the basement, dozens of eyes were on them. Among them were Maria, Peter, and the kitchen girl whose name he didn't know but remembered well from the Rooster. And maybe at this moment, when their eyes met, he briefly considered what he was doing, but only for a moment. Because Mara spoke for him, he didn't need to explain anything.

"This is Tim. He used to be a gatekeeper and let me through, but now he's here, wanting to join us!" And that was it. He was neck-deep in the resistance. He couldn't have devised a better plan if his goal had been to infiltrate. Sure, some looked at him with disapproval, but Mara's faith convinced them. Tim's confidence grew, and he felt more at ease in this new role.

Throughout the evening, there was light-hearted chatter and beer. The most awkward moment was when Maria asked Tim what was in the briefcase. Tim had thought about explaining this but had yet to come up with anything. So, the question caught him off guard.

"Unfortunately, I don't know. Judith, my former partner who helped me cross over, the briefcase was her business. I just accompanied her. She has already gone back," Tim replied, barely thinking about what he was saying.

"So, you know a gate where you can go back?" asked a stocky, stubbly man whom the others called Guldar, and it seemed to Tim that he might be some decision-maker here.

Tim nodded mysteriously at the question, and Mara kissed him on the cheek as if proud of how useful a person she had found for the team. The team's acceptance of Tim was palpable, and he felt a sense of inclusion he hadn't experienced before.

"But you can go back too, right? I assume your contracts aren't permanent?" Tim mused aloud because he had to admit that what he knew about the team or the local situation was practically nothing.

Guldar responded, "Returning means completing a full screening and inspection once our contracts expire. For instance, if you want to carry something forbidden, you'd need a gate that the authority is not monitoring. How you talked about your partner suggests you know of such an illegal gate." Tim was starting to understand the intricacies of the situation, and his knowledge was growing.

"Yes, but it's a very delicate situation, so you need to fill me in on all the details..." Tim smiled awkwardly.

"You'll learn everything tomorrow; we're just relaxing now!" Guldar said happily, ordering another round of drinks.

"Out of curiosity, what was your plan if I hadn't come along? If I understand correctly, you want to smuggle something out," Tim pried.

"We have another plan, but it's not safe at all, for example, using tourist papers to get back, but there's a high risk of getting caught. That's why an unmonitored gate would be better. We know there are such gates on the island, quite a few actually, but we haven't found a way to access them yet..."

"When you came to the restaurant with the woman, you were wearing lab coats..." Peter interrupted. "We suspect there's such an unofficial gate in the lab where they're working on the new teleporter. Is that where the one you know is?"

Tim started to realize why they trusted him so much. It might not just be Mara but also the circumstances.

"Yes, but I can't reveal my contact. If you want to smuggle something out, I'll take it through if you like, but that's all I can help with."

He could see that the team was satisfied with his answer. Tim suspected they wanted to smuggle out the invention's plans and was utterly confident they couldn't obtain them. From Zack? No way!

As the atmosphere lightened, proportional to the amount of alcohol consumed, Tim chatted more freely. He was somewhat restrained about what he could share and avoided revealing what he knew.

But when they talked about the little girl they were still searching for, and Guldar and the others believed she had likely been caught and killed, Tim couldn't hold back.

"The girl has already gotten out; she's fine. My partner and I found her, and she took her through that gate," he boasted, and as soon as he said it, he knew he shouldn't have. Maria smiled, approached him, and hugged him.

"Although I had doubts about you, this convinces me!"

She plopped down on the couch beside him, kissed him on both cheeks and started wiping off the red lipstick marks. "Come to the restaurant tomorrow; we'll make you a burger or whatever you want!"

Now, sitting between two girls, Tim smiled. Maria urged him to tell them everything about the little girl. The elimination of her father was undoubtedly a significant blow to the resistance. But Tim saw that the girl's rescue filled them with hope.

Tim recounted how they found her and evaded Dash, omitting that the incident was entirely accidental. From his account, the others might have thought that Judith and he knew where to find them but could only save the girl.

"But you can't tell anyone about this!" Tim grew serious. "My partner is working over there to ensure the authorities don't find the girl, to hide her with a new identity completely. If this gets out, they would start searching, and you know cameras are everywhere. I'm already worried that my partner might fail, and they might find them..."

Everyone nodded and agreed that this secret would accompany them to the grave.

"Dash has been a thorn in my side for a long time... so it was them..." Guldar began. "Who isn't working tomorrow? How about a little scuffle?"

Everyone raised their glasses in agreement except for Maria, Peter, the kitchen girl, and Mara. Tim was still determining because he had no plans for tomorrow while the girl worked at the hotel.

Guldar observed how hesitant Tim was, unsure if he was free. "Come on, Tim. What's holding you back from a little revenge if you're not working?"

Tim shifted uncomfortably: "Mostly, I'm here incognito. I have to go back Sunday night. I didn't want to draw the authorities' attention to myself."

Guldar smiled at him with satisfaction: "No one will pay attention to you; we know their every move!"

"The authorities? Do you have informants there, too?"

"If you mean agents, no. Much better than that. We work here, Tim. We are the unnoticed cleaners, repairmen, doormen, whatever you want, who get everywhere. For example, I clean at the residence of their big boss..." Guldar winked.

Suddenly, Tim made sense of the similar small soaps at the restaurant and Zack's. "That's brilliant!" Tim cheered, feeling antsy and finding the two remaining days excruciatingly long. "So, all the workers here are part of the resistance?"

"No... I wouldn't say that. But one of the supply companies exclusively employs people from the resistance."

This explanation cleared up a lot for Tim. And if someone were to ask Tim what he was doing at that moment—gathering data for Zack or genuinely being a member of the resistance—he wouldn't have a clue. At that moment, he just wanted to survive the next two days.

The group started to pack up around midnight. Some had already left earlier, like those who worked at the Rooster, as they needed to rest. The streets of the small resort village were still bustling with activity.

Tim put his arm around Mara, and they walked behind the others, heading to a dance club. Tim just went with the flow. He saw couples around him: Guldar and a tall, thin girl were walking ahead of them. The girl wore high heels and had to bend down to talk to the much shorter man. There were two other couples with them, about whom Tim knew almost nothing. One girl mentioned working at a gas station, and Tim tried to recall if he had seen her before. Her partner was a mechanic, but they needed to specify what they worked on. Maybe cars?

There were hardly any cars on the island; most people used small electric scooters. Or nothing at all. Tourists generally stayed in one place, enjoying the sea and their accommodations. They didn't need much else. The island wasn't a place for active vacations, although there were mountains in the island's interior that could be suitable for hiking. However, because of the lab, these forests and cliffs were off-limits to tourists. The beach remained the only place for relaxation.

Tim knew nothing about the other couple, which sometimes bothered him, but they seemed more familiar with Guldar, so he assumed they must be colleagues.

The place they arrived at was packed. On the dance floor, Tim felt like a sardine. But Mara wanted to dance, so they mostly held each other and swayed to the music.

Then Mara pulled him outside, and the fresh air was a relief. He could finally hear something. The others had disappeared, and they walked home together. Tim felt he was in the right place and wished this day would last forever. He had never partied and had a girlfriend with whom he just wandered.

He wanted to savor every moment, but Mara was a little worried because she had to get up at nine in the morning. So she asked Tim not to be mad, but she had to say goodbye.

Tim suddenly finds himself alone among the strolling tourists, feeling lost because he doesn't know where he is. It must have been around four in the morning, and it took him a while to find the right direction back to his lodging.

He collapsed onto his bed, fully dressed.

Chapter 18

As the first light rays emerged from behind the horizon, the sun began its majestic ascent, casting warm light upon the earth. Its brilliance gradually spread, illuminating every corner, including Tim's room, as he had unfortunately forgotten to pull down the blinds when he collapsed into bed at dawn. The sweet sound of birdsong filled the air as the feathered creatures awakened to a new day, their melodies harmoniously blending with the tranquil atmosphere... yet something seemed off, Tim thought, still dreaming, because there were no birds here. Or were there only no birds in Heine?

In this half-dream, the rhythmic melody of the waves gently caressed the shore, orchestrating a symphony of calm and wrapping the environment in a serene atmosphere. Tim felt that everything was good around him. He thought of checking on Mara and waiting for her outside the hotel to greet her, but he wasn't sure what time she started work. And Tim didn't want to seem weird. So, after thinking this through, he fell back asleep into this strange dream of waves and birdsong, waking up only at noon. He remembered that Maria had invited him for a hamburger, so that became his goal for the day, and he also recalled something about a confrontation they had agreed upon—against Dash.

Around noon, he walked into the restaurant with a pounding headache, and when Maria saw him, she laughed and said something like, "If you can't handle alcohol, why drink so much?" There was some truth to that, but he didn't want to reveal that he rarely drank.

In the restaurant, he sat in the same spot he used to with Judith. For the first time, he thought of his boss or former boss. He hoped everything was fine with the girl and there wouldn't be any trouble.

As he pondered this and drank his coffee, he marveled at the two older adults at the counter, who always seemed to be there. The lady now seemed to be knitting something different, a different color, but he wouldn't have sworn to it. When Maria came back out, she sat across from him. "So, a hamburger? You liked it quite a bit last time!"

"Yeah, and do you happen to have any headache pills?" Tim squinted.

"Sure, I'll bring some... and Tim! I'm glad you're with us!" the waitress smiled at him.

"These folks," Tim gestured around. "Are they always here? Are they part of the staff, too?"

"Well, something like that, they keep an eye on us." Maria stood up and rummaged behind the counter, returning with some tablets. Meanwhile, Tim imagined the old lady protecting Maria, and then it struck him that there might be something to it because the last time she handled that weapon quite confidently, it was likely still hidden in her knitting bag.

"Do you get other guests besides them?"

"We're usually full, but our reputation has taken a hit due to supply issues," Maria apologized.

"I vaguely remember agreeing to some brawl. With Guldar and his crew?"

"Yeah, you did," Maria laughed. "I think they'll be here soon, too; they usually have lunch here when they're not working."

Then Maria brought out his hamburger, and Tim reminded the one Judith had eaten in the car. When he got into the car that day, he could still smell the onions; maybe he should clean it.

The same taste, only this time, he didn't have to rush. He savored the food and even managed to eat his fries. The world was nearly perfect. When he ultimately finished his meal, Peter came out to greet him. Seemingly, he just wanted to say hello and express how glad Tim had joined them.

"Guldar will fill you in on the plans for tomorrow. He may want you to accompany us; we'll transport the item tomorrow. I'm off work tomorrow, but unfortunately, I can't join you today..."

"Oh yes, something about a scuffle," Tim nodded, beginning to feel better.

"Do you know when Mara finishes?"

"Well, she's working a twelve-hour shift on Saturdays, so she'll be done by 9 PM. But you'll probably find her in the basement after that. You remember the place from last night. That's where we usually hang out."

Tim thought the basement was a fitting name. Then he remembered something else. "And tell me, how did you manage to get across? I was worried when the inspectors dragged you out of the line..."

"Oh, don't even mention it! I nearly had a heart attack. I thought you had snitched on me. But it turned out they just pulled everyone whose destination was Heine. My papers were in order, or at least they thought so. But I still needed help to cross there, and then I found a gatekeeper in Farlington who would let anyone through for the right price. Once in Heine, I managed to join the staff legally."

"That was lucky! After that, they kept a close watch on me, but fortunately, I got an assignment just in time, but let's leave it at that..." Tim found it hard not to be honest because Peter seemed likable and had a winning manner.

"Mara mentioned that you want her to go with you on Sunday because something is happening after that?"

"Yes, it's a long story, but she could get into big trouble, partly because of me, since I let her through." Tim tried to give convincing reasons why he was so insistent on Mara going with him. And Monday is my deadline."

"So, they're looking for her? But she's working legally, she has papers, a job..."

Tim felt he needed to explain more. "I can't say much more... but you should lay low here too. Something's brewing... they caught your big boss, and their goal is to silence the whole organization. My cover is in danger, having a name in the system that I let through despite it being prohibited."

Peter understood and nodded. "If we succeed with our plan and manage to handle the invention, our organization's presence here will become unnecessary. We can practically dissolve the whole thing."

This line of reasoning reassured Tim, and apparently, Peter also accepted Tim's explanation. Peter then went back to work, although no new guests arrived. Tim didn't have to wait long for the others; he had just finished an apple pie when Guldar and five other young men walked through the restaurant door. They sat down with Tim, joking about whether he was ready for a little scuffle. Guldar always referred to trouble as a scuffle.

As they ate, Guldar tried to brief him on the plan and left Dash a message to meet them there.

"Here? You mean in the restaurant?" Tim was astonished. He couldn't think of a worse plan.

"Of course, here. You've got a weapon, right?" asked Guldar.

"Yeah. But why not in the forest or some deserted place?" Tim protested as he didn't like this plan. He remembered the previous scuffle here, which they only avoided because Judith talked their way out of it. What if things went wrong this time?

"Here, because people like Peter are working, they can join in on the fun too..." Guldar laughed. "Hey Maria!" he called out. "That Dash guy, I called them here, so you'll be in on the action too."

Maria came closer. "Are you going to trash the restaurant? Or what's your plan?"

"Why, are you the owner or something? Nobody comes here besides us anyway; it's on some blocklist..."

"That's true, but we need a concrete plan. If we start shooting here, well, I don't know, someone might survive. Your partner was right the other day."

"And now we're back to square one..." Tim shook his head, as he didn't like this new setup at all.

Plan or no plan, they argued so long that the group surprised them in a tense atmosphere without a solid plan. Dash, wearing black sunglasses, came in first, followed by his four companions. They stopped at the entrance and scrutinized them.

Tim had earlier tried to position himself with his back to them and placed the old lady and the always-reading gentleman behind the counter in front of him. He had a plan. Shoot as quickly as possible, giving Dash no chance to reveal anything about him or

Judith. But his main plan was to ensure they didn't get out because if Zack found out what was happening here, it would complicate his life on the other side, or especially here.

And now he realized he hadn't even planned what would happen after Sunday night. They would still have to hide if Mara went with him and they started a new life. But the level of hiding and the reasons they would seek mattered. So his caution was justified, he reassured himself.

"Do you want to finish what you started here last time? But it looks like a few more of you now, aren't there?" Dash grinned and pointed outside, where men in identical suits were loitering, seemingly without reason, as if they were coincidentally standing in the small square in front of the restaurant.

Tim cautiously placed his gun in front of him and unlocked it, noticing Guldar's nervous gesture to hold off for now.

"But you came prepared..." Guldar began. "And how do you know we aren't even more numerous?"

This assumption threw Dash off a bit. He pushed his sunglasses up onto his forehead and stood with his hands on his hips, confidently waiting. "So, what do you want? Why are we here?"

"There's a little incident, a story about a little girl whose parents you killed. And now we know it was you... We are here for revenge or a lesson; call it what you want."

"So it is true, the resistance hotspot. I thought you had the sense to disappear by now. Do you think the authorities aren't already on your trail? That they don't know who you are? In a few weeks, the whole organization will be dismantled!" Dash shouted.

And that was it. Tim stared intently at Guldar, then at the two elderly folks behind the counter, just waiting for the stocky man to nod finally. But Guldar hesitated for some reason, and Tim didn't like that. Finally, the old lady looked at him, and Tim involuntarily gave the signal. After that, everything happened so quickly that the five men at the entrance couldn't even draw their weapons. But they weren't the more significant problem; the ten to twelve guys started moving in at the sound of gunfire.

Tim found shelter behind the counter, beside the two elderly folks, figuring this was the safest spot. Everyone fired from behind cover, and he heard the kitchen's glass door shatter, with gunshots coming from there, too. The worst off were likely Guldar and those seated at the table. Judging by the silence from that direction, it didn't bode well for them.

The old lady was surprisingly decisive. Plenty of bullets were beneath her knitting needles and yarn; if anyone was prepared, it was her. She and the older man fired in excellent coordination, taking turns. Tim knew he had decided to jump over the counter before the massive hail of bullets began. He felt a bit sorry for Guldar, but he had his chance to devise a better plan.

"Is there a back entrance?" Tim whispered to the older man.

"Yeah, from the kitchen...It's a good idea to get behind their backs! Go ahead, we'll cover you," he said, and they both started shooting.

Tim quickly ran towards the kitchen and, to avoid being riddled with bullets, shouted as Maria peeked out to shoot, "I'm coming through!" Maria nodded and stepped aside from the doorway.

"Where's the back entrance? We need to surprise them!" he shouted, relieved to see Peter there and the kitchen girl whose name he really should remember, especially since she guided him.

The plan worked surprisingly well. While everyone was shooting towards the main entrance, Tim and the girl picked them off one by one from behind.

Chapter 19

T im impatiently waited for the others in the basement, especially Mara, as he was worried the authorities would uncover all the members' names and workplaces. Tim's sole purpose here was this girl, Mara; the rest didn't matter to him. After the shooting, he rushed back to his lodgings, making sure he wasn't followed. Essentially, he spent the entire afternoon peering out the window, watching for any suspicious figures.

And then there was the anxiety. If he check on Mara, would he put her in danger? And what was Guldar's actual goal with all this?

When Peter arrived, this was his first question to him. "Man, don't ask me such things," Peter defended. "All he told me was that we're taking revenge."

"But, strangely, he planned the shootout in the restaurant if that's what he wanted," said Noeme, the kitchen girl whose name our protagonist had finally learned.

Meanwhile, Mara also arrived, and they had to explain everything to her. The tall girl, Guldar's girlfriend, cried and drank. Karl, who somehow survived the whole thing, was sitting at the table from which Tim had fled just in time, and he presented an interesting theory: "I don't think Guldar wanted a shootout. He didn't give any signal for it; our new friend, Timothy, started the whole thing!"

Tim's suspicion was growing like a storm. He glared at Karl. "Of course, he gave a signal; he looked at me and nodded. Isn't that a signal?"

"You pulled out your gun; Guldar only gestured to wait!" Karl shouted. "I think he had completely different plans!"

Tim fumed. "Different plans? Like what? Do you think we would have just chatted about the weather? It was about revenge!"

"Tim is right," Maria interjected. "Dash wouldn't have been satisfied with a little chat. That's why he came with so many people. If they had started the shooting, even fewer of us would have survived!"

Karl's hate-filled glare at Tim was a clear sign of the tension in the room. "Now, we should focus on completely lying low. The organization is dissolved from now on!" Several people murmured at Peter's words. "After today's stunt, I think it's logical."

"What about the meeting with the inventor tomorrow?" Karl asked, his voice tinged with worry.

Tim was also very curious about this part. He was almost sure Bernardt wouldn't hand over the description since he saw him discussing it with Zeck unless this was about something else. "Are you sure it's not a trap where they'll catch you?" Tim asked.

"Sure! Bernardt is a good guy; he already sold us the prototype, but the authorities somehow found out where it was and reclaimed it. Guldar was the contact, but fortunately, he briefed me too, so I know where he'll hand it over tomorrow."

"I'm still almost certain you're walking into a trap. I think it would be better to let the matter rest a bit," Tim said.

"That's not an option since you're crossing over on Sunday evening. It's our last chance to get it through with you. If Bernardt does hand it over, and you're right about it being a trap, we need to get rid of it as soon as possible so they don't find it on us," Peter thought logically, but Tim still wanted to find a way out of the whole thing. He wanted to spend more time with Mara because he hadn't yet figured out if she was as attracted to him as he was to her. She had returned his kiss and was sitting beside him now, but Tim was growing increasingly doubtful. The fact that his appearance came in handy and that he was now entrusted with the invention made Tim a useful member, but he also felt used.

Would the girl still sit next to him if he hadn't promised anything?

And how could he find out? While he was lost in thought, he didn't notice that the others were already talking about how, with the restaurant gone, the employees—Mara, Peter, and Noeme—would have to go into hiding because they would undoubtedly be watched. They needed to acquire new identities and jobs quickly. Tim thought this wouldn't be difficult as they had their connections.

Mara kindly offered to let them stay at her place tonight since her apartment was large enough. That evening, they stayed briefly, and everyone left individually.

Although Tim had other plans for Mara, he had to be satisfied with the girl hugging him and assuring him that they would meet tomorrow and that she was ready to cross over with the invention.

"And if there was no invention? Would you still come with me?" Tim whispered in her ear. Mara looked surprised and just stared at him with her big brown eyes. She said nothing; she slipped out of his embrace and followed the others. This silent rejection did not reassure Tim.

Only Peter and Karl remained in the basement, finishing their beers. Tim envied Peter for spending the night at Mara's apartment and began to have strange thoughts about whether they knew each other better. After all, Tim barely knew anything about the girl.

Peter wrote down an address for both of them. "Be there at eleven. Don't come by car and act like you were passing by. Bernardt will hand over the description to me, but it would be better if you cover me if it's a trap. For example, it's a park, so you can pretend to be jogging. He'll be sitting on a bench; I'll go over, he'll hand it over, and that's it. Watch to see if he's alone or if someone is watching. If you see anything suspicious, one of you come over and ask if we know the time. Once I have the pen drive, I'll try to pass it to you."

"Now that's a plan!" Tim said. "Much better than Guldar's chaotic approach!"

Karl glared at him angrily, but Peter interjected: "Let's not start this now; there's no time for it. If anything goes wrong, the pen drive is the key! Tim, ensure I get the description across if something happens to me! I'll write down my contact's name. Look for them, and give it to them!"

Tim felt the world spinning around him. He suddenly had the power to bring down an entire network.

Suppose he decided to stay on as an inspector with Zack's team. But he was primarily worried about whether Bernardt would hand over the description. And how should he dress so the inventor wouldn't recognize him?

Then, as he walked home, the fresh sea breeze blowing, he suddenly felt calm. There wouldn't be any handover; that Goat-bearded man couldn't be that crazy. They would go there, no one would be there, and then he would cross over with Mara in the evening. What other choice did the girl have? She had to hide here, too, with the resistance disbanded. Everything would be fine, he reassured himself.

Still, the old dream about Mara returned that night. He was standing knee-deep in a swamp, and when Mara walked past him, she just waved at him with a smile and kept walking, not even stopping to help. Yet Tim was struggling, trying to escape the heavy mud that wouldn't let him move.

He didn't know what this dream meant, but it left him in a bad mood, and he woke up early.

Mara was working that day, and in the morning, as he got breakfast, he headed to the hotel. He walked as he had taken Peter's advice. As there were so few cars, everyone knew whose was whose.

He saw the girl walking alone toward the hotel, which reassured him. Until the meeting time, he was occupied with finding the right running outfit, one in which he wouldn't be recognized. The main thing was the hat, but since his distinctive ears stuck out of everything, he finally bought a blonde wig with a neon green headband, tucking his ears under it.

He looked terrific, and he was satisfied with what he saw every time he looked in the mirror. Even Karl didn't recognize him; he was warming up by a tree when Tim walked by. Tim mimicked Karl's movements, making Karl think he was some odd character, so he moved away. The situation amused Tim, who continued to clown around until Karl was furious. "Relax, it's me!"

Karl looked at him with wide eyes, impressed by his running outfit. He hadn't gone overboard, wearing shorts, running shoes, and the same T-shirt as yesterday.

They warmed up by walking a few laps around the small square. There were benches along the path, and soon, Peter was sitting on one of them. They didn't see anything suspicious. With the sun blazing above, this was the time when people preferred cooling off at the beach rather than jogging or sitting in the city's small park, so there was no one else around.

To Tim's surprise, Bernardt showed up. From a distance, he recognized the annoying face with the goat beard. Bernardt was carrying something strange under his arm, which looked like a dog at first. As he got closer, they saw it was a cat, the kind without fur and very wrinkled.

When Bernardt got close to Peter, he put the cat down on the ground and handed something over. Then he walked away with his ugly cat on a leash. That was the handover, and Tim couldn't believe how simple it was. Peter waited, stood up, bent down as if adjusting his shoe, and walked away.

"Did Peter say where we'll meet next?" Tim asked. He wanted to talk to him to determine if the description was on the pen drive.

"At Mara's place, she finishes at four today."

He gave Tim the address, and they went their separate ways.

Tim had grown to like this running outfit, especially how the headband hid his ears. He ran down to the beach, where he barely found a spot to sit due to the crowds of sunbathing tourists. But Tim was determined and wanted to swim again before leaving. He didn't mind that people stared at him strangely as he walked onto the beach in his neon green running gear, only taking off his shoes and shirt before running into the blue waves. He swam far out again, losing the wig at some point, but he didn't care.

At home, he ate some leftovers, regretting that he couldn't have a hamburger today. Then he remembered there must be other restaurants but wanted to avoid drawing attention to himself.

After four, he headed to Mara's place. He found himself going with the flow again. His main goal was to go back with Mara and start a new life together if that's what she wanted. And that was what he needed to find out.

Peter opened the door, and it was clear he was ecstatic.

"We did it! You hear? We did it!" he cheered, even hugging the emotional Tim.

"Did you check? Is it on there?" Tim asked.

The room wall projected complex engineering drawings and formulas they didn't understand, but it also depicted a portable teleporter.

"Let's raise our glasses to Mara and Tim, who will take the invention and end the authorities' monopoly on teleportation!" Maria cheered.

Mara also appeared as excited as everyone else. Only Tim was lost in thought, mainly puzzled by the inventor. Why did he sell his invention to the resistance? Was Bernardt also a sympathizer of the organization? Was he shamelessly outsmarting Zack, who greeted him as a good friend? Tim thought they knew each other very well. And the fact that Bernardt didn't like him from the first moment—they mutually disliked each other. And when he remembered the cat...

So, while the others celebrated, Tim pondered two things. First, how can he find out if Mara loves him and will come with him even without the description? He was sure there wouldn't be any invention, and it wouldn't be an issue. Second, Bernardt irked him. He found himself concocting plans to warn still Zack, which was utterly irrational since he wouldn't have time. The plan was to head straight to the lab with Mara. Just the two of them, meaning he could talk to Mara. Could Jimmy pass a message to Zack? Could he ask him to do that?

CHAPTER 20

Events unfolded quickly, and soon they were sitting in the car with Mara, the smell of onions still lingering. Tim hadn't had time to clean it, and Mara was slightly uncomfortable, trying to clean the seat under her and wondering where the smell was coming from.

It was evening, and Tim could have considered this little trip romantic under different circumstances. They were driving through the forest on a winding road, and Tim didn't remember having to grip the steering wheel this tightly and focus so much on the road. The situation complicated his plan to calmly discuss everything on the way to Jimmy's place.

Tim began his speech as he had planned. He started from the moment he first saw her and fell in love. "I've never seen a girl more beautiful than you, and your smile simply captivated me. You must know that I would never have let anyone through the gate. I always do my job properly."

"Tim, we barely know each other! And you're already talking about love; it scares me," Mara said worriedly.

"So you think it's too soon? Because I came over for you to ensure nothing bad happened to you!"

"You were worried about me? That's so sweet! But you also came because of the resistance, right? To help us," Mara said, watching Tim maneuver to avoid falling into the ravine on the dark, narrow road.

"Uh-huh... but you were the main reason," Tim replied. He continued when they got past the dangerous section, "When you came and tried to bribe me, if someone else had been there, would you have smiled at them as kindly?"

"What do you mean? Oh, you're asking if it hadn't been you? But we only met then. If it had been someone else, I would have tried to bribe them..."

"But would you have smiled at them too?" Tim pressed.

"I don't know what you're getting at... I smiled because I wanted to make a good impression so you'd let me through," Mara replied, annoyed by Tim's silly questions.

Tim didn't want that answer; he wanted to hear that she liked him too and that there was some connection between them from the start.

"But Tim, I like you, and I hope we stay in touch on the other side too..." Mara tried to smooth things over.

"Yeah, I know you like me, but I'm worried, and I know it's silly, but I keep thinking, would you still like me if I wasn't useful to you?"

"You mean, did we use you? But you don't seriously think that, do you?"

"I'm just wondering if, if I weren't a dedicated member of the organization and we didn't share the same goals, would you still like me?"

Mara shook her head. "I don't like how you're acting. You're talking in hypotheticals; what if this or that? What are you getting at, Tim? You haven't changed your mind, right? You know how important it is to the organization that we get the description through!"

"Yes, I know, but I did all this mainly because of you. I came over because I was worried about you. I want to believe in love, and if you don't love me the way I love you, I need to know that..."

"I like you, Tim. You're a great guy, but I'm not in love yet; it takes more than that. Do you understand?"

So he found out what he wanted, and he thought it would hurt a lot more. He even felt slightly relieved because now he didn't have to decide.

"But this doesn't change the plan, right? You haven't changed your mind, have you?" Mara asked, worried.

"No, of course not. I always keep my promises," Tim reassured her, feeling himself becoming more distant from her. They were almost where they had stopped last time, though it was hard to tell in the dark. It was a dirt road now, with walnut trees on both sides.

The dark forest seemed intimidating, and Mara felt a bit nervous, but seeing Tim moving forward so confidently, she hurried after him, trying to keep up with his fast pace.

Tim just wanted to get this over with. He was serious about finishing what he had started. They would return, Mara would disappear with the description, and he would return to his tedious gatekeeping job.

Jimmy appeared at his door again with a gun, as if he had a sensor buried somewhere in the ground to alert him.

"Ah, you're here," he lowered his weapon and let them in. "Judith told me you'd come tonight, Tim, and that you'd bring a girl! Great, you found her; I'm happy for you!"

Tim started to take off his shoes, but Jimmy stopped him. "Leave them on. I'll clean up later. You'll need to put them back on when we go to the teleporter anyway. But first, rest a bit and tell me what's been going on," Jimmy smiled encouragingly at them.

"I don't know how much I can tell you or how much Judith told you... maybe it's best if you don't know anything..."

"After what happened last time, nothing would surprise me anymore," Jimmy admitted. "I understand if you need to keep secrets, but I ask you to forget about this gate forever! Seriously. If I ever see you here again, or if you send someone else here, I'll shoot without hesitation. I won't even ask questions!" It was clear he meant it.

"That's understandable, and I'm sure she will also promise. I know you've already helped more than anyone could expect."

Mara nodded. "I wouldn't even know where we are exactly; we came in the dark..."

"Good," Jimmy was pleased. "I didn't want to spoil the mood, but we must be clear. So, I assume you need fake papers, too?"

"For the girl, yes. But I'm returning to the gatekeeping, so I don't need them. Just erase my movements," Tim said.

Mara stared at him with wide eyes as if she wanted to say something but then decided against it in front of Jimmy.

To Tim, the tunnel from Jimmy's closet to one of the small rooms in the lab seemed much longer this time. Mara walked ahead, and as he watched her blonde hair, he realized he didn't even like it; the brown suited her much better. It was as if he had found a completely different girl here.

It was painful to realize that Judith was right after all. As they moved through the dark spaces, he even thought that he didn't want any of this; why bother taking the girl across? Nothing made sense anymore.

Then he remembered that he had promised and couldn't go back on his word now. And the invention's description? How could he stop it? How could he take it from Mara? His head hurt from all the dark thoughts. He debated the most about whether he should stay here with Zack's team. Going back could have made more sense; what would he do there? Judith wouldn't be far away, and boring gatekeeping might no longer satisfy him. He might always wonder what would have happened if he had stayed.

When they entered the giant hall, it was empty again. "Does this laboratory even work?" Tim asked, but more to himself. Jimmy heard him and answered while searching for the key to the small room: "When experiments were ongoing, yes. But the inventor doesn't come here anymore; why would he, since the work ended? Now, it's just about guarding the documents and leftover materials. But there used to be a lot of activity here; this lab was operational for twenty years. I remember when things were so secretive that we got the order to tape up all the windows. Then, once the invention was ready, everything stopped overnight."

"You're talking about Bernardt, right?" Tim asked. "I met him; somehow, I find him very unpleasant. I can't explain why."

"Yeah, that's him. He has his quirks, that's for sure. He had a cat he took everywhere, even here, and its food cost a fortune. It didn't eat just any cat food, only salmon."

In the meantime, they entered the small room, and Tim felt uncomfortable being close to Mara. It's strange, he thought, how much things have changed. While Jimmy fiddled with the papers, they waited in awkward silence. Jimmy had already arranged for Noir to open the gate on the other side; they had nothing to worry about.

Then, in front of the gate, Mara pulled Tim aside. By then, Tim had more or less decided that Mara would go with the description as planned, but he would stay and join Zack. Mara's words surprised him: "Tim, I can see that you no longer trust me, that something has changed in you. I'm sorry you expected more, but we can determine what might be between us once we cross over. Okay?" She looked at him with her big brown eyes, and Tim almost felt that feeling again, that he would do anything for her. Mara continued, "I want to regain your trust. Take the description; you bring it!" With that, she reached into her pocket and placed the pen drive in his hand. "I'll wait for you on the other side, okay?"

Tim stared at the girl and the small pen drive, gasping for breath. Jimmy said that Mara could go.

The girl started, gave Tim an encouraging smile, then stepped into the bluish swirling light and disappeared.

"In a moment, you can go too," Jimmy said, punching codes into the teleporter.

"Jim, can I quickly check what's on this pen drive somewhere?"

"Sure, in the small room over there, but hurry back."

Tim didn't trust Mara? The girl had seen this very clearly. Until this moment, he had been stewing in his thoughts about how foolish he had been to join the resistance. The pen drive contained the exact description and the same images. So she had given it to him? He stood there with the small device in his hand; suddenly, his thoughts changed. He went back to Jim. "I'm not going after all; things have changed."

"Really? So suddenly?" Jim lifted his head.

"Yeah, sorry!"

"What should I tell Noir? Or will you write something to him?"

"Can you write to him that I've changed my mind? I'm staying and ask him to help the girl disappear."

Did Tim think about how the girl would feel when she realized what happened? Yes, and he somehow felt a sense of satisfaction that it was only fair to return the bad feeling she had given him.

As he returned to the car, he felt a bit guilty. But only for a moment. He imagined Mara, or whatever her real name was, crumbling when she realized she hadn't managed to get the description across. Tim consoled himself by thinking the girl should be happy that he let her escape, and he deliberately didn't ask for her new name to ensure she wouldn't think of finding him later. He had enough craziness with the resistance, and Bernard still bothered him.

He was tired when he reached his quarters at dawn. He was glad he had the chance to start a new life here, one full of excitement. And he was delighted the Mara issue was over, that he no longer behaved like a madman. Only now, looking back, did he see how blind he had been.

The usual dream caught up with him again, but he walked quickly into the swamp this time. He ventured deeper into the dark, swampy forest; the girl was nowhere to be seen, and in the sky, he saw dark, thick clouds. There was no trace of a blue sky.

When would these dreams end?

Tim approached Zack through the main entrance this time, but the same thing happened: he was surrounded and checked.

This time, the doorman didn't take him to the dining table but straight to Zack in a smaller room.

"Timothy! I'm glad you're here! Are you ready to join my people?"

They shook hands, and Tim placed the pen drive between them on the small coffee table. "How much do you trust Bernard?"

Zack was surprised by the question. "I've known him for quite a long time; if you look at it that way, we're friends."

"That's not good news. This pen drive contains the description of the invention. Bernard himself handed it over to the resistance."

Zack picked up the small device and signaled to his man at the door. He projected it with the projector, and Zack's astonishment was evident. "How did you get it, and how do you know he sold it?"

"In the past two days, I infiltrated the resistance a bit; I was there during the handover. I prevented them from taking it and brought it to you. And I suggest you screen the cleaning staff because some resistance members work here too."

Tim handed over the names and everything he knew except for Mara. At least he stuck to his promise; he didn't want to break it.

After discussing everything with Zack, he received his first task. To kill Bernard.

CHAPTER 21

Bernardt's story begins when he meets Tim at the long dining table at Zack's place. He is nervous because he never goes anywhere without his cat, but he cannot bring it to Zack's because Zack is allergic to cats.

His cat was completely hairless, so he hardly understood how his boss was allergic. When Zack first saw his beloved Katy, his eyes started to water, and he sneezed, which was a typical allergic reaction. He had to leave the cat alone in his beachfront villa. Of course, the staff was there, but Katy considered them intruders and would jump on them from various places, scratching their clothes. She had even scratched one cleaner's face, so they had to ensure Katy wasn't home when the staff was working.

So now the cat was all alone, making our inventor very irritable. He fiddled with his phone every minute, watching the live feed to see what his little Katy was doing. His irritation wasn't helped by Zack keeping him waiting, and he was seated at an uncomfortable dining table. He couldn't understand why there wasn't a waiting room with a sofa where people would comfortably be waiting. Moreover, a strange guy in a lab uniform had joined him.

The lab had been closed for a long time, and there might only be guards there, so how did someone get a uniform? Could Zack be spying on him? Were they inspecting the lab?

He had done everything to ensure Zack wouldn't suspect him, nodding when asked to stay on the island. Even though he had finished the work, the teleportation device was ready. He understood that the authorities needed this small teleportation device because they funded its development.

However, despite being given a luxury villa on the beach, he had difficulty accepting that he felt like a prisoner and no one could tell him when he could leave. The beautiful surroundings only highlighted his lack of freedom, making him feel more trapped than ever.

He had expected something else. Maybe fame? Recognition as a great inventor, with his name living on, like Professor Walnut, who even had a village named after him. He had started developing, or instead improving, the teleportation gate so that teleportation would be available to everyone, freeing them from government control. But look, things hadn't turned out as he imagined; they wanted to keep this device under their control too, and that's why they were holding him here, despite the luxurious surroundings making it seem like a reward.

And that's precisely why he sought contact with the resistance. He had already sent the prototype to them, but something must have gone wrong because now Zack had summoned him, and the agent with Zack had a black briefcase just like the one he had handed over. They couldn't find out he had willingly given it to them; Max had promised that no one would find out what happened. They believed the resistance had stolen from him. So, he wasn't worried about the briefcase, but the lab uniform concerned him.

Bernardt was fidgeting nervously, thinking about barging into Zack's office and telling him not to mess around with him. Why summon him if he was going to keep him waiting? What would he say—that he had an urgent golf game? It better not mention the cat since Zack hated cats.

Finally, the glass door opened, and Zack greeted him loudly. But first, he introduced the person waiting with him—Tim. What an idiotic name! And how rude to barge in ahead of him.

After the unpleasant incident, Zack finally attended to him. They shook hands, but he noticed his boss's eyes were already tearing up, and he sneezed twice.

"Man! I can smell the cat on you! Eventually, I won't be able to summon you because of the scent in your clothes..."

"We could talk over the phone. I wouldn't have to come here in person..." Bernardt tried to negotiate, as it would also be better for him not to leave the cat alone.

"That's not possible; everything is bugged. And it's not just one resistance group we have now; they're popping up like mushrooms." He sneezed twice again.

"Bless you!" Bernardt said, but Zack just wiped his eyes and nodded in thanks. Bernardt couldn't help but feel a twinge of guilt. Zack's allergic reaction was a constant reminder of the sacrifice he had to make for his work.

"I'll keep this short because this is getting awkward. It's about the prototype. Did you know it was stolen and ended up with the FYI organization?"

"Stolen from the lab? But it's guarded! How on earth did that happen? You said nothing could be taken out of there. They didn't even let me in!" Bernardt tried to feign surprise, his heart pounding in his chest.

"Yes, yes, but that's not the point. My two people here have retrieved it, so it's back with us." He pointed to the black briefcase.

"Oh, well, that's great! But why did you summon me?"

"There are certain rumors that you helped get this briefcase to the resistance. Of course, I didn't believe it for a minute. However, I would like to request documentation for the teleportation device. I want to keep it to ensure it doesn't leave the island." Zack's words only fueled Bernardt's growing suspicion.

Bernardt didn't like this situation. "Yes, I have it all documented. I can give it to you, of course." He knew he was only safe if he cooperated and did everything they expected of him, a realization that made him feel even more trapped.

"Great. I won't take up any more of your time. Can you bring it tomorrow?" Zack sneezed again.

"Sure, or rather no. You see, I need to review it and add a few calculations. The final touches... to make it clear for an average scientist too... I'll be here with it on Monday morning..."

"There aren't any copies of it, right? I don't want any copies. I want the original and only document!"

"Of course, of course!" Bernard nodded and wondered if Zack was allergic to him, not the cat. And what if Zack only found him helpful as long as he had the document? If he believed the rumors? And once he handed over the document, would Zack have him killed?

With these thoughts, he got into the car sent for him. He didn't drive himself, and the driver was very talkative. On the way there, he had asked all sorts of questions about his cat, and Bernardt had chatted amiably then. But now, he wished the driver was far away and pretended to have a terrible headache to avoid conversation.

Bernardt stepped into his house with a trembling stomach, sensing that his cat would be angry for being left alone for so long.

He headed straight to the kitchen to open a treat, hoping to make amends.

"Katy!" he called, holding her small bowl. Nothing, not even a sound. It seemed she was upset, poor thing.

The cameras on his phone were motion-activated, set to switch on when there was movement. He couldn't remember why he'd configured them that way, but it seemed logical not to disturb the camera while the cat slept. As he toggled his phone, no motion was detected, so he had to check the rooms himself.

But he stopped short in the living room. The first thing he noticed was the curtain and the drapes. When he had left, they were still hanging on the windows, but now they lay on the floor, shredded to pieces.

The curtains and his favorite armchair, where he watched his favorite shows, were torn apart. The armrests and cushions were slashed beyond recognition. How could such a small cat cause so much destruction?

"Katy!" he called again, more impatiently this time. The cat was still nowhere to be found, and now he started to worry. He frantically ran through the rooms, only to hear a strange noise from one of the bathrooms. Opening the door to the powder room, he almost fell back in surprise. Katy was sitting in the toilet bowl, clinging with her front paws, unable to escape.

Bernardt quickly lifted her out, not caring that he got soaked. The poor cat was trembling, barely able to make a sound.

"What happened? Were you being naughty? Didn't I tell you the bathroom is off-limits?" he said, grabbing a towel from the cupboard to wrap her up and dry her off. Katy hated water, always needing a tranquilizer for baths.

Looking into his cat's eyes, he saw the reproach in her gaze and knew it would take a long time to make it up to her. He had already forgotten the chaos in the living room.

He checked her body and legs for any injuries. "Does anything hurt? I know you hate the vet, but I must call her!"

Katy meowed as if she understood what was coming.

"What happened here?" asked the vet when she saw the wrecked living room.

"I had to leave her alone, and it seems she didn't handle it well," Bernhardt explained.

"Did you give her a tranquilizer? You know I won't go near her without it." She only moved when Bernardt nodded. "Don't get me wrong, but she has behavioral issues. It would help if you thought about some things. This cat takes up all your time. My niece, who you went out with once, keeps asking when you'll call her back. What was wrong with her? You can tell me now!"

"Ahh, you know, Katy didn't like her..."

"That's what I'm talking about! This cat isn't normal! She fell into the toilet bowl. And how couldn't she get out?"

Daniela approached the cat cautiously, knowing she was sedated. She also checked her thoroughly. "She's fine! She could have gotten out if she wanted; she's strong!"

"Her paws slipped on the wet tiles, and she might have been shocked. You know she hates water!"

"Shall I help bathe her while she's still groggy?" the doctor asked.

"Yeah, could you? I'll order something for dinner. Are you staying?"

"I'd love to, but I don't want to be around when your cat fully wakes up. Who knows what state she'll be in? She might not spare you either."

"Oh, come on, she's a sweet little cat, usually very gentle. I've just left her alone a bit longer than usual," Bernardt explained as he carried the cat to the bathroom.

With her practiced hands, the doctor finished the bath in no time, or perhaps she just hurried to leave as quickly as possible.

At the door, she paused for a moment. "Please call my niece. I don't want her nagging me. You owe me that much!"

Bernard nodded, but the truth was he barely remembered the girl. He briefly pondered this, thinking the doctor might be right since he had cut off all his human relationships to give Katy a peaceful life.

But he couldn't help it. He couldn't do anything but melt when he looked into those big, intelligent, black eyes. This cat was no ordinary feline—very smart, almost as if it could speak. And yes, he had considered how the toilet incident happened and why it couldn't get out. But he didn't want to think further because animals couldn't be so clever as to manipulate their actions.

He sat on the couch where Katy was lying and petted her clever head. The cat opened her eyes and looked at him reproachfully, making Bernardt immediately realize he was in trouble. He quickly brought some treats.

A few hours later, when she finally accepted the food, he could sit and calmly think over the day's events.

Max, his contact who had helped him sell the prototype, came to mind. He realized at Zack's that he should also give a copy to the resistance. If something happened to him, the invention would be in a safe place, ensuring the world would know about it. He increasingly believed that once he handed it over to Zack, he would have him killed. Especially if Zack finds out, there is a copy.

He called Max during petting the cat, who seemed to have completely forgiven him.

"Max, are you sure this line is secure? It is not eavesdropping?" Bernard asked.

"Did you call from the phone I gave you?" came the reply from the phone.

"Yes, yes, so it's secure. Okay, listen, I'm calling because I was at Zack's today, and he said the prototype is back with him. And he mentioned hearing some rumors about me, that I sold it. I'm in big trouble. He might have already hired someone to kill me. I must disappear. Can you help with that?"

"I'll call a few people, then let's talk tomorrow, okay?"

"Thank you! And Max, I'm counting on you! Please don't let me down! And one more thing, I want to give a copy to the resistance, too. Arrange a meeting with them as soon as possible."

"You're critical to the resistance; I'll do everything possible!"

"Okay, thanks!"

He felt a bit calmer but still had thoughts running through his mind, so he immediately started making two copies.

CHapTer 22

Bernardt always envisioned a world where teleportation was a free form of travel without the need for complex official permits and various approvals. The last straw for him was the introduction of the EPRS number, a regulation that further hindered the use of teleporters. It only served to keep travel even more under the authorities' control.

He dreamed of making this travel safe and accessible anywhere, even in distant places in space. When he shared this plan with Zack, he was initially enthusiastic, but after discussions with the leaders, they raised numerous legal concerns. So, nothing came of it, even though Bernard had already worked out the theoretical part. This rejection is why he started to build connections with the resistance. The system is flawed if the authorities don't want to progress and give space to new things. And he no longer wanted to be a part of it.

What prevented him from leaving the little island earlier and joining the resistance? Simple. No one wants to go into exile voluntarily. His current life was very comfortable; he had everything—a luxury villa and a beautiful ocean view—or rather, that's all he had. Despite the millions of ideas racing in his mind about how his invention could make life easier, the authorities would never want the development.

For instance, as he stood in his room looking at his favorite armchair scratched to pieces, he thought that ordering a new one and having it shipped by boat would take several weeks, maybe even a month. Teleportation would make it so much simpler. However, transporting objects or even food by teleportation was strictly prohibited due to legal issues. However, he felt it still required authorization primarily because of opposition from big transportation corporations.

So, it was utterly pointless to order a new one; if all went well, he would be gone in a few days anyway. Until yesterday, he was afraid to join the resistance openly, but now he saw he had no choice.

In the mornings, he usually took his cat down to the beach; they walked and looked around while the cleaners did their job. Katy's favorite carrier for these occasions was a backpack with a pouch part at the front, from which she could stick her head out and enjoy the wind hitting her face as they sped along on the electric scooter.

Katy's favorite activity was riding the scooter to the beach and walking there. Bernardt always got a coffee and sat on the beach promenade, watching Katy try to catch the little crabs, who quickly ran back to the water as if they knew the cat wouldn't follow them.

On this day, Bernardt had another plan besides drinking a coffee and tiring out the cat. He wanted to buy a new collar with a holder to hide a pen drive. Now that he had the new portable teleporter description on three pen drives, he kept all of them with him because he didn't trust his staff. One would go to the resistance, one to Zack, and one to Katy's collar.

Katy wasn't pleased about not going straight home, meowing disapprovingly from the backpack when she noticed they weren't taking their usual route but heading towards the supermarket instead.

"Shall we get you a pretty little collar? Would you like that?" he said encouragingly, kissing the cat on the head.

After a long search, he finally found what he was looking for. He bought a rhinestone collar because Katy liked shiny things, particularly the black rhinestones. He also found a men's necklace with a small pouch that could hold anything. He would remove the pendant from the necklace and attach it to Katy's new collar. Bernardt even tried fitting the pen drive inside, which fit perfectly without being noticeable.

Katy gracefully accepted her new accessory and purred as if she was rewarded for yesterday's chaos. The cleaners had done an excellent job removing all traces of the mess, putting up new curtains, and getting rid of the armchair.

He spent all day waiting, impatiently checking his phone for Max's call to find out what he had managed to arrange. He hoped Max understood how important this was. Katy must have sensed his impatience as she stopped before him and meowing, which she didn't usually do. Then, when the much-awaited call finally came, she sat on his lap and meowed randomly into the phone conversation.

"Bernard, I've got good news!" Max began. "They're expecting you in the park at 11 on Sunday. You can hand over the description there. The contact will be sitting on the fifth bench from the entrance. Does that work for you?"

"Of course, of course. And the other matter?" Bernard asked, trying to calm Katy, who seemed to be having difficulty with her owner's attention not being on her.

"That one was a bit tougher. There's a gate at the lab, you know it too."

"Yes, but it's impossible to get in there now. It's guarded like a fortress."

"To the right of the entrance, there's a dirt road through the forest. Follow it, and you'll reach a small house. Jimmy used to work in the lab; you might know him. He's a caretaker or security guard now. But he takes his job very seriously. Unfortunately, I've had to ask him for favors several times recently, and he's gotten pretty grumpy. So if he gets irritated, don't mind it. He's a good guy, just protecting his skin. When he found out who it was for, he softened up. But he made me promise never to send anyone to him again."

"I'm grateful you arranged it."

"I hear you still have that annoying cat. But you're not planning to bring it with you?"

"Don't joke; she's like my child. And listen, if something happens to me... the cat has something important..."

"Do you feel like you're in danger?"

"Yes, you know, I'm going to see Zack on Monday; I am a bit concerned about what will happen next, but if all goes well, I'll go to your Jimmy, and everything will be fine."

The Sunday handover in the park went smoothly, and Katy behaved well. She was calm as they walked to the park the whole time, and Bernardt carried her in his arms. And he made a surprising discovery. While they were walking in the park, two joggers passed by them. He was worried that the cat would jump out of his arms and something would go wrong, but quite the opposite happened. The tall blonde in a ridiculous neon green running outfit looked at the cat, and Katy purred back. This connection was something he had never encountered before. His cat only purred for him, yet this strange figure just had to smile and win over his cat.

On the way back, he pondered this, wondering if perhaps his cat was changing and becoming much calmer. The doctor had also said that eventually, as she aged, she would shed her quirks. He just needed to be patient. He had patience, so since he considered himself a good inventor, he applied scientific methods and experimented.

They went into a shop with Katy, who was not in the backpack. Well, that was a mistake, as she immediately jumped onto someone's back, who started screaming. They could only catch the crazed cat with the help of a security guard, who cornered her.

So she hadn't calmed down; it was just that young man who had triggered something in her? On the way home, he looked at the cat suspiciously and felt jealous.

He was very nervous about the Monday meeting. It also stressed him out that he had to leave the cat alone in the house again, not knowing what kind of madness she might get up to. The other source of stress was Zack himself. Would Zack have him killed right after the handover? He hoped for a little more time, or Zack still didn't suspect anything.

Katy looked sadly at him as he prepared to leave. She only got suspicious that her owner would leave her alone again when he left a treat in her bowl, much more than she usually got.

"I'm just leaving you for a little while. Be a good girl, okay?" he stroked and kissed her forehead.

He didn't dare look back because tears rose in his eyes. What if this was the last time he saw Katy? And did he only feel sorry for his cat in this world? Maybe Danielle was right, and this wasn't good.

Zack was sneezing again when they met.

"Not again!" he said, pulling out a mask. "This may help"!

"Let's make this quick. Here is the description," Bernardt said, handing over the small black pen drive.

Zack took it and turned it over in his hand. "Are you sure there are no copies of this?"

Bernard was about to speak when he noticed Zack placing it on the coffee table beside an identical pen drive.

Undoubtedly, this was the one he had given to the resistance. But how could they be so amateurish that both the prototype and now the description had ended up with Zack?

"Do you want me to make excuses? Do you want me to come up with some good pretext?" said Bernardt, realizing after a quick assessment of the situation that he could do nothing—he had been caught red-handed. All he needed now was to buy a little time.

Zack stood up, sneezed a few times, and poured two glasses of whiskey. He never usually offered Bernardt a drink because he knew the inventor didn't drink, but now he did, and the inventor accepted it.

"Bernard, I don't know what drove you to betray me like this and twice at that. I've always done everything for you and stood by you. So I want to know why?"

"I am grateful for everything, and I know the invention wouldn't have come without your support. But Zack, you're putting the whole thing in a drawer! I didn't work for nearly 20 years for the world not to know who I am and what amazing thing we've created here!"

"So it's about fame?"

"Not just that. It's more about having my invention used and brought to market to replace the old gates with something entirely new and more practical. To make it possible to travel with a watch-sized teleporter. That's why I worked for so many years! And you know, I have more ideas. We could use it in space travel as well. The technology is already there."

Zack impatiently waved his hand. "Yes, I understand, but Zack, it's not the right time yet. The government needs to regulate everything. Otherwise, there would be anarchy..."

"If satisfied with this, we might as well return to the Stone Age."

"But you haven't joined the resistance, have you? We're in the process of dismantling the entire group. I'd hate to see your name on one of the lists..."

Bernardt, though tempted to voice his opinion about the government, realized it was better to stay silent if that still counted for anything. "No, not that. They just approached me, and the possibility of fame blinded me. That's what happened..."

Zack took a thoughtful sip of his drink. "It's a pity it turned out this way because I liked you. You can go."

Bernardt didn't move yet, looking at the drink in his hand, and slowly sipped it down. He stood up when Zack started sneezing again.

He knew he was in big trouble, and if he got out of the house alive, someone might be waiting for him at home with a loaded gun.

He anxiously got into the car that had brought him. But he had no choice. "Could you drop me off at the supermarket? I just remembered I need to buy something for my cat," he said to the driver, who just nodded—this time, they hadn't sent the chatty one to pick him up.

He tried to blend in the supermarket and constantly watched to see if anyone followed him. Then he thought about the cat and how to get her without being noticed. Finally, he decided to send someone else for her. He hurried to the doctor's office, who was surprised to see him without the cat. "But she's okay, right? Or did you finally get rid of her like I suggested?" she asked.

"I am in big trouble, and I need your help," Bernardt said, looking out the office door to see if anyone suspicious was around.

"What's gotten into you? You're scaring me!"

"Listen, they want to kill me, and I need to disappear quickly."

"Jesus, what have you gotten yourself into?" the doctor exclaimed in shock.

"Could you bring Katy here? It's crucial! And also my electric scooter and the backpack next to it?" Bernardt took both her hands in his and put them on his heart, pleading with her.

"Katy? And what if I can't catch her?"

"You must have some way to sedate her. Don't you have a tranquilizer gun?"

"You watch too many adventure movies! I'm just a vet on a vacation island, not in the middle of the wilderness!"

"Please! Could you try? If you put the sedative in a treat? Please, help me. I can't go home because they're watching my house!" He looked at the doctor with such a miserable expression that she felt sorry for him.

Cursing herself, Daniella was soon sitting in her car, holding a treat soaked in sedative.

CHAPTER 23

Bernardt thought he should have prepared better for this great escape while waiting in the doctor's veterinary office. For example, he had packed only the essentials in his small backpack, which were related to the cat: her favorite food, treat, and vitamins. It only now occurred to him that he hadn't thought about himself—he hadn't even packed an extra pair of underwear.

At the moment, he was just glad to be alive and hoped Daniela would manage to bring Katy. If he had thought through the situation more, he could have planned for the possibility that he might be unable to return to the house. But it was too late to think about that now.

Suddenly, he realized they hadn't clarified what would happen after he teleported. And where would he go? So he called Max and hurriedly asked his questions. "I could have asked these earlier, but I can't think straight now. It's only now that I've calmed down and thought things through," he apologized.

"I understand, but there's no need to worry about that. But tell me, when are you leaving?" he heard Max's surprised response.

"I still have to take care of something in about one or two hours, but definitely by the evening."

"Alright, hurry up. You'll teleport to Walnut Grave, where you'll first get a new identity. A good friend of mine, Noir, will be waiting for you. He'll take you to a safe place to stay for a few days without attracting attention. If everything goes well, I'll come to get you myself. So everything will be fine, don't worry about anything," Max reassured him.

"I won't have much with me. I couldn't pack clothes for myself..."

"That's okay, but you'll need a new photo taken for your new ID, so you should change your appearance.

"Oh, yes, I hadn't thought of that..."

"Alright, see you soon, and please hurry!"

Bernardt felt somewhat relieved, glad that he had called Max. Although they had never met, they had developed a relationship where he trusted Max with his life.

The veterinary office was empty, and as he paced impatiently, he saw his gaunt reflection in the mirror above the sink. Yes, recent events had worn him down; it was no wonder he couldn't concentrate and kept forgetting things. In this exile awaiting him, it might be necessary to shave off his beard or style his hair differently to avoid recognition. And if he had gone home, he would have taken care of these details.

He stared at his carefully groomed beard, which he could shave off. This beard was so much a part of his identity that he might not even be recognized without it. Out of the corner of his eye, he saw a pair of scissors and began cutting it off. He didn't think about whether he would miss it or how he would look without it. It was tricky to cut it neatly with scissors and shape it so that only stubble remained. He spent almost half an hour making it look as precise as possible and was very satisfied with the result. He was about to start restyling his hair, having gotten into the mood of transforming himself, when the doorbell rang.

Bernardt was delighted that his cat was finally here, but when he looked into the waiting room, a man in a suit stood before him, carrying a large pointer dog.

The man stared at him in confusion, as if he hadn't expected this. "I'm looking for the doctor. Is she here?"

"She had to run an errand but should be back in a few minutes. I'm waiting for her too," Bernard replied, only now realizing he still had the scissors. He quickly put his hand behind his back to hide the tool and, to ease the awkwardness and distract himself, asked, "Did something happen to the dog?"

"Yes, he must have stepped on something during yesterday's walk. But we only noticed today that he was limping badly, and when I checked his paw, it looked pretty bad..." He set the dog down on one of the chairs and lifted the dog's left hind leg, from which a small piece of metal protruded. It needed to be more apparent to Bernardt how a dog could step on something that would pierce its paw unless it had accidentally jumped from a height and landed on that shard. The dog whimpered in pain and licked the tall man's face.

"It's quite nasty, actually, but I'm not a doctor, so I can't help," Bernardt apologized.

"Can't you call her? He's been suffering long enough..."

Bernardt should have called Daniela to see what was taking her so long, but he didn't want to disturb her because he knew how difficult it could be to catch Katy. He often couldn't manage it himself when the cat got stubborn. Fortunately, he didn't have to ponder or decide as the doctor angrily walked into the waiting room, helmet in her hand and pushing the electric scooter. The backpack hangs over her shoulder.

At first, Bernardt didn't understand what was happening, but when Daniela handed him the backpack and the helmet, he began to understand.

"Sorry, but I couldn't catch that damned beast. She didn't even look at the soothing treat as if she knew what it was. I tried everything!"

"So you left her?" Bernardt was stunned.

"Yes, I did—that devil. Your curtains are shredded again, and your sofa is in tatters. Just forget about that beast!"

"Excuse me! Could you help my dog?" interrupted the man in the suit, who was trying to hold his dog on the chair so that the injured leg wouldn't touch anything. The dog was quite heavy, and the man was losing his patience.

The doctor decided she was done with Bernardt's case and wanted to turn her full attention to the distressed dog. Naturally, Bernard wasn't pleased with this, as he was practically scared to death.

"Can you bring him into the exam room?" she said after taking a quick look at the nasty wound and the protruding metal piece.

The man hoisted the dog onto his shoulder and followed the doctor, who put on gloves and prepared an injection. Bernardt watched from the doorway, following them.

"Daniela! I wouldn't have asked you to do this if it were unimportant! I can't go home, understand?" Bernardt pleaded.

"The dog is getting a shot now, which will ease his pain; I'll try to pull out the metal piece. Good dog!" she said, then turned to Bernardt after giving the injection. "I told you, I tried everything. As soon as she saw me, she tore up the curtain. I watched, and after she finished with the curtain, I put the treat in front of her, but she just stared at it and then at me. After that, it was the sofa's turn."

"So what should I do now?" Bernardt was shocked.

"Why can't you go home?" the stranger joined the conversation.

Daniela and Bernardt stared at the man as if they had just noticed someone else there.

"That's a long story, not important," Bernardt waved off, preventing the doctor from blurting out anything. She had already said too much.

"There's only one solution—you have to go yourself. I can't do more to help. The soothing treatment is still on the floor. If you're lucky, your cat might have eaten it, and you can easily catch her," said the doctor, focusing on the dog's paw. Bernardt still stood there helplessly, holding the helmet in one hand and the backpack in the other, missing Katy.

"What is this thing he stepped on? A metal piece?" the doctor asked.

"Yesterday we were walking in the forest; something must have happened there, but I only noticed today that he was limping..." the man replied.

"Very strange, it looks like a bullet, but it's shattered," the doctor speculated, already pulling it out with tweezers and holding it up to the light.

"Bullet?" the man was also surprised.

"Yeah, see its shape? Very strange. Where did you walk? Did you hear about the shooting at the Rooster Restaurant?"

"Yes, it's terrible what's happening! Do you think it needs stitches?" the dog owner worried.

"Can't you go back?" Bernardt asked impatiently, checking his watch. "Maybe she ate it and is lying there, dazed..."

"Bernardt! I have work to do, can't you see? I need to stitch up this nasty wound. And what did you do to your beard?" The doctor finally noticed the inventor's new look. "Can't you ask someone else?"

The truth was, he couldn't. And this stranger, who seemed to be watching with interest, had already learned too much. Bernardt took a deep breath, resigning himself to the idea that he would have to return to the house, where someone might be waiting for him.

"Did you see anyone suspicious around the house?" he asked as he decided to go back for Katy himself.

"No, no one. You're acting so strangely today, Bernardt!" said the doctor, but Bernardt didn't listen. He grabbed the helmet, fastened it to his head, and, without saying a word, left the room with the electric scooter.

That was it; he had no choice. Maybe he would be lucky and wouldn't find his assassin there, or perhaps they wouldn't send someone until tomorrow.

As he sped along the road, conflicting feelings swirled inside him. Would he still return for Katy if he hadn't put the USB drive on the cat's collar? Yes, definitely. He shook his head. The thought itself was offensive. How could that cross his mind now? He knew his cat was problematic, but he believed she would outgrow her quirks, and besides, she could be a sweet little cat, too!

Was it worth risking his life for her? He would only answer yes to that, and he started worrying if the hitman would kill the cat, too. This thought made him stubborn. No, he wouldn't leave his clever cat.

He no longer cared about the invention or even his own miserable life. All he thought about was Katy, hoping she was safe.

As he maneuvered around the many tourists on the boardwalk who were disturbed from their post-lunch stroll by a speeding scooter, he felt a growing determination and strength. Whatever he found at the house, he would handle it. The key was to believe in himself, that everything would be alright.

Although drops of sweat beaded on his forehead from the stress, Bernardt only thought positively, repeating like a mantra that everything would be fine.

CHAPTER 24

Bernardt left the electric scooter on a side street because he wanted to be cautious. Though he didn't mind looking strange, he kept the helmet on his head. He watched from a distance to see if anyone was in front of his house, but nothing seemed suspicious. A car was parked further away, but there was no movement inside. When he had gathered enough courage, he headed towards his garden gate to enter from the back.

He entered the house and couldn't believe it, but everything seemed fine. Of course, the living room was in terrible shape, just as the doctor had described. The curtains were torn and lying on the floor, and his sofa was scratched up, with bits of stuffing poking out here and there. A piece of the treat was in the middle of the living room floor, meaning Katy hadn't eaten it. He knew it was pointless to call for the cat since she never responded to that. As he looked towards the kitchen, he saw the "beast," as Daniela had called her, sitting on the kitchen counter, seemingly calm. She meowed sweetly and looked at him with the expression she had when she was in her excellent kitty mood.

Fighting back the tears, he walked towards the cat, picked her up, and hugged her tightly. He was unable to talk due to a lump in his throat. He felt relieved, believing nothing wrong could happen now—they were safe. He was opening his backpack to put his beloved cat inside, who was already purring, when he noticed something on the kitchen counter he hadn't seen before.

On his marble-topped, pristine white counter lay a black silenced gun. Shocked, he froze and started listening intently for any sounds. But where was the gun's owner? When he heard the toilet flushing from the bathroom, he panicked and instantly knew that the person Zack had sent was there. He didn't understand where he got the courage or determination, but instinctively, he picked up the gun and turned toward the bathroom.

Tim stepped out of the bathroom, and now it was his turn to be shocked. Bernardt immediately recognized him as the guy who had strutted around Zack's place in a lab coat, and it hit him that Tim was also the neon-clad runner in the park. Katy greeted the hitman with a friendly meow, which filled Bernardt with such fury that he didn't fire just once; he emptied the entire magazine into the dumbfounded, tall, big-eared boy.

Gasping for breath, he dropped the gun onto the counter and carefully put Katy into the backpack. At that moment, he also realized they must have been watching him when he handed the plans to the resistance. He now understood why Zack had the description.

Still wearing his helmet, he adjusted it slightly and, feeling like he had taken care of everything, stepped out the door and hurried towards the electric scooter.

The car parked further away must have been Tim's, and it only now occurred to him that it would be more practical to take the car, especially for the forest road. The car reeked of onions, and as he suspected, the key was left inside. He hated driving, but he knew it would be much faster than using the electric scooter, which might need recharging.

Katy didn't feel good either, wrinkling her nose and nudging Bernardt's chin with her head. "It'll be faster this way, you'll see. Just bear with the smell a little longer! I won't take you out of the backpack; it's safer for you this way," he reassured the cat as he fastened his seatbelt carefully, ensuring it didn't squeeze the cat on his chest, just him.

He started shakily, needing to get used to how the pedals worked, particularly how much pressure to apply to the gas pedal. To his surprise, the gas pedal was very sensitive; a slight press made the engine roar to life. Or maybe he was just too nervous?

So they were on their way, and he started to take off his helmet with one hand, tossing it onto the back seat and focused intensely on the road. He was gripping the steering wheel too tightly, approaching every intersection cautiously. "When will we get out of the city?" he asked, to which the cat responded with a meow, patiently watching as her owner fumbled around.

If she could talk, she would probably have commented on his driving, told him to speed up, or asked what he was doing. And Bernardt, even without words, understood what Katy was thinking and replied to her: "I know, but understand. I haven't driven in over ten years. If you think you can't forget how to drive, you're very wrong."

Then he remembered how friendly the cat had been with that Tim kid. She was usually distant and incredibly hostile with strangers. "You weren't a good cat today. Did you let that guy in? You even purred at him? What got into you?" Bernard asked, but Katy just watched the road with her intelligent eyes. It was as if she sensed her owner's uncertainty, keeping an eye on all the other cars and the many pedestrians. Finally, they left the crowded holiday area and headed towards the mountains.

Bernardt felt like he could breathe for the first time, thinking they were on the right track now; they just had to survive these very winding roads. He drove cautiously, perhaps overly so, when another car caught up to him from behind. At first, it just came too close, indicating it wanted to go faster, but because of the successive bends, it didn't dare to overtake. Then, seeing that Bernardt wouldn't speed up, it started honking, making Bernardt more nervous and even more cautious.

To the right of the road was a dizzying drop, and on the left was a cliff face. If someone came from the opposite direction, there wouldn't be much room to maneuver, and he could easily fall into the ravine. The height terrified Bernardt, and he couldn't understand why the driver behind didn't see the danger or where he was in such a hurry to get to.

Thinking more about it, he realized he was also in a hurry but valued caution much more. After going through so much, he wouldn't risk his life to get there a bit sooner.

But the car behind him was in a hurry and wasn't concerned that they were on a dangerous stretch of road. The driver leaned on the horn, trying to get Bernardt to go faster, but since Bernardt couldn't be convinced even by that, the driver made a surprising maneuver and started to overtake him. What bravery, thought Bernardt, holding his breath as he watched, hoping no one would come from the opposite direction, and curious to see who this jerk was who couldn't control himself. When he looked to the side, he saw it was the man from the veterinary clinic. They stared at each other for a moment, and finally, the annoying car overtook him and sped ahead. Then Bernard saw that it braked, and now he was following them, noticing that besides the dog owner in the passenger seat, there were two others in the back and the driver.

Then they braked so hard that he had to stop, and all four of them got out of the car in front and approached him. Bernard didn't know what to make of the situation, but when he saw four guns pointed at him from all directions, he started to suspect he was in trouble.

"I guess I celebrated too soon!" he said worriedly to the cat, who meowed in response.

They opened his car door and gestured for him to get out. Bernardt unfastened his seatbelt, and, with the cat sitting in the backpack on his chest, he got out with his hands raised, staring at them in confusion. He suspected they had recognized him; perhaps he had talked too much at the doctor's office. The dog owner was one of Zack's men.

"Where is Timothy?" asked the dog owner.

"Who?" Bernardt stammered, then glanced at the car and suddenly realized whose he had taken. "Oh, I don't know. The car was in front of my house, and I needed it, so I stole it because the keys were inside... but that's not such a big crime, is it?"

"He's lying!" snapped the guy with glasses. "You're the inventor, aren't you?"

"He is, Bernardt," replied the dog owner.

"Tim was looking for you, and you're driving his car. That's a bit odd," the guy with glasses continued.

"Let's talk to Zack and see what he wants to do with him; we'll take him with us in the meantime," the dog owner said.

"But why? Why not just shoot him and be done with it?"

"We don't know if Tim needed to get something from him."

Bernard felt as if things were happening independently of him. These four armed guys were calmly discussing his fate among themselves. Just when he thought things couldn't get worse, he was in the worst life situation. How would he get out of this? And if everything were true, he would end up back with Zack. They shoved him into the car, put a bag over his head, and tied his hands in front of him.

They drove for a while; he first felt they were on the road, then on a much bumpier path. It must have been a dirt road because the car bounced around, and he swayed back and forth inside. When they finally stopped, they pulled him out of the car and, still with the bag over his head, led him somewhere and down some stairs. A musty smell hit his nose, indicating they were in a basement.

They sat him on a chair, and only then did they remove the bag from his head. By then, Bernardt had lost all hope and knew it was the end. The cat in the backpack on his chest was peering around. He only had one last hope: if the cat managed to escape from here and was lucky, she might end up in good hands, along with the invention. That was all he could think about as he saw that only three guys were with him, waiting, while the fourth must have been talking to Zack.

The room was nearly empty, with a table on the corner and a single bulb hanging from the ceiling, which they turned on. Confirming they were indeed in a basement or semi-basement since there were small, long windows near the ceiling, one of which was open. Carefully, Bernardt raised his tied hands to loosen the backpack strap. Katy sensed she could escape the backpack's trap; she had been fidgeting for a while. With one leap, she landed on the ground and, before anyone could react, jumped onto the table and then on one of the small window sills.

But it wasn't the one that was open. The guy with glasses raised his gun and aimed, but the dog owner grabbed his hand. "Leave it, it's just a cat!"

The third guy, leaning against the wall, lit a cigarette and stared indifferently at the cat, and Katy also eyed the three men from her perch.

Bernardt didn't know how to signal the cat to escape through the open window, but there was no way to signal her. He could only hope that his smart cat knew what to do. But Katy just sat there and started licking her fur.

EPILOGUE

Bernardt began reassessing his situation and the unfortunate turn his life had taken in the last few hours. When the fourth guy in a suit returned, all his hope vanished.

"Zack wants us to get the name of your contact in the resistance," he said, putting on a pair of mechanic's gloves from his pocket. "It's up to you whether you tell us nicely or we beat it out of you."

"I still have to go back for that dog, so we should make this quick," the dog owner said, pulling off his suit jacket and rolling up his sleeves in preparation for the beating.

At first, Bernardt didn't understand or didn't want to understand their preparations, but he couldn't have any illusions; the guys were serious about extracting the information from him. He had no doubts; he suspected that even if he told them, they would kill him anyway. Was he afraid for his life? That day, he had crossed himself secretly several times, so he felt prepared for the inevitable. Resigned to his fate, he stubbornly refused to say anything.

No one would learn any names from him.

"So, who did you give the prototype to, and later the plans?" the guy with the cigarette squatted in front of him, drawing imaginary circles in the air with the cigarette between his fingers. Then, with a sudden move, he pressed the lit end of the cigarette against Bernardt's hand.

It hurt a lot, but Bernardt tried not to make any noise other than a hiss. He was thinking that Tim had been there when he handed it over. Did they know who he gave it to? Or do they want Max? He definitely wouldn't give up Max; if Max were exposed, it would end the entire FYI.

"I see you don't want to cooperate," said the dog owner, and Bernardt received a punch from the right. The blow split his eyebrow, and he felt the blood run down his face. The force of the punch knocked him off the chair, and two of his interrogators lifted him back onto it.

And it went on like this—they kept hitting his face, he sometimes fell to the ground, they lifted him again, then shouted at him if it wasn't enough yet, and that he just needed to say a name.

But Bernard held out, even though he could barely see, and everything hurt. Once, when he fell and lay on the ground, leaving there a bit longer to let his beaters catch their breath, he caught sight of Katy, who was watching. She was still standing on the ledge, but at least she was no longer preoccupied with licking her skin; she was watching what was happening.

At that moment, it seemed to Bernardt that he saw something in the cat's eyes, something like madness, or he wasn't sure what. And then he was back in the chair, now with a gun pressed to his temple, threatened to be shot if he didn't give a name. Bernardt couldn't take his eyes off Katy, who was preparing for something, as she flattened her ears and got ready to pounce.

But what did she want? And then, as if in slow motion, he saw his cat lightning-fast at the throat of the guy holding the gun, slashing his face and chest with incredible speed, then leaping to the next one, scratching each of them with her claws.

All four of them writhed on the ground in pain, unable to see because their faces were covered in blood and flesh wounds.

Bernardt slowly came to his senses from the sight, and Katy, as if satisfied with her job, stood before him and meowed once. She was like saying, "Okay, we can go now; what are we waiting for?"

Bernardt stood up, limping because they had also kicked him when he fell. He had the mind to pick up his backpack from the floor. He opened the door and, though with difficulty, climbed the stairs. The cat patiently walked beside him, skillfully avoiding his path whenever he stumbled so he wouldn't step on her.

The car was still there, even the door was open, and when he got in, and Katy sat on the passenger seat, he finally looked around, unsure of where to go because he had no idea where he was. And with his hands still tied and a swollen, bleeding eye that made him see only vaguely, how was he going to drive?

The whole situation seemed so hopeless that Bernardt started to despair when Katy meowed as if urging him to get going.

"So, you're saying I should just go, and that's it? But where?" He looked around and saw that there was no key. This was a modern car, probably with some fingerprint or retina scanner. He had no idea, and when he realized this, he screamed in frustration.

But Katy seemed to understand, placing her paw on his thigh as if to say, "Come on, let's go."

"On foot? Or how?" With no other choice, they got out of the car and started back down the dirt road. The cat was leading in practice, with Bernardt trailing behind, holding his backpack. It was getting dark; he should have been at Jimmy's long ago.

Then the cat suddenly turned off the dirt road, walking through the forest for a long time, as if she knew the way, and her owner just followed her, having no idea where they were.

Only when he started seeing more walnut trees did he begin to hope, and when the grey building of the lab emerged from behind the trees, he began to relax. Katy had found her way home. After all those months of bringing the cat to his office daily, she knew the way.

Jimmy, standing in front of his small wooden cabin with a gun in hand, didn't concern him much. He hurried towards him, and the cat followed as Jimmy helped the beaten inventor inside.

A few hours later, after a bit of washing and some wound cleaning, Bernardt began to feel a bit better. Jimmy was constantly grumbling.

"How am I supposed to photograph your face like this? I'll have to do a lot of retouching. And what about the cat? You know you can't go through together, right?"

Jimmy kept talking and expressing his doubts, but secretly, he was glad to be part of the plan to rescue the inventor and aid the resistance.

Bernardt still couldn't believe what had happened to him. When Jimmy took the photo for the ID and asked for a name, he thought of that peculiar figure, that tall guy whom Katy inexplicably liked, and said, "Make it Timothy; I'll leave the last name to you."

"Alright. Could Katy be the first cat to teleport?" asked Jimmy.

"I don't think so. We've done various experiments with animals. Katy herself has used this, though only within the building."

"I thought animal experiments were banned..."

"Officially, yes." Bernardt smiled, nostalgically looking at the old teleporter and Katy, who had come to him as a test subject but had something special about her that made Bernardt keep her.

"They're completely shutting them down, these old models. So it's just in time that I'm sending you through." Jimmy handed him the ID.

Katy went first, knowing exactly what to expect. When the bluish light appeared, she bravely walked into the swirling blue.

"Thank you for everything!" Bernardt said as he bid farewell. "I hope we meet soon on the other side."

"We will. Sooner or later, I'll get out, too."

It was Bernardt's turn, and with a bit of sadness, he left the lab so dear to his heart, where he had worked on his invention every day for twenty years. So many failures and sleepless nights!

The bluish light of the teleporter glowed, and he disappeared into the vortex.

Noir was waiting for them at the other end of the teleporter. At first, he didn't know what to make of a cat coming through, but then he saw that there would be one more jump. Katy waited patiently for her owner, and when she saw him, she jumped into his lap to greet him.

"How secure is this place? Because Max said he's coming here too."

"There's no more monitoring since teleportation has completely ceased, much to the locals' delight. This teleporter will be dismantled within days..." the old man lamented.

"So, we're completely safe here?"

"For now, yes, there's no one from the authorities here. But you look awful. It looks like you've been beaten up!"

"Yes, there was some fighting, so I was late. I appreciate you waiting for me."

"Is it true that you're the inventor who made that wrist-watch-sized teleporter?" Noir scrutinized Bernardt.

"Uh-huh. Yes. I'll have to redesign it since I couldn't keep the prototype. But I have the plans, so I need the materials."

"Wonderful! You'll have the time and space for everything here. It is peculiar that Professor Walnut also built the first teleporter here. Sadly, they want to demolish it. But never mind, it's high time the new one replaced the old one. I can temporarily house you in the previous gatekeeper Timothy's place."

Meanwhile, they arrived at the tiny house via back roads through the forest. "I live across the way," Noir said, pointing to his home. "If you need anything, just let me know."

Upon entering the gate, Katy immediately jumped out of his lap and started sniffing the grass, cautiously approaching a pile of clothes. "Tim wanted to make a scarecrow out of it because birds were pecking the seeds from his garden."

"Wow! Tim did some gardening too? Interesting." Bernardt bent down and picked up the coat rack. He could already see what a great scarecrow he could make. "So, there are still birds here?"

"There are, not as many as before, but there are some."

Katy was chasing bugs and soon disappeared among the bushes. "Did you know this Tim kid well?" Bernardt asked.

"Pretty well. Tim was a perfect kid, but something happened to him. I blame myself because he was so close to seeing that the authorities' excesses weren't realistic. The problem is I should have guided him, but I let him make his own decisions. Then, poor girl, just yesterday... She came over, waiting for Tim, but he didn't show up; he took off with the plans. It's a shame. He fully committed himself to the authority, and since we don't know how much he might tell them, we did not protest against the destruction.

Katy appeared with a mouse in her mouth and dropped it in front of them. She looked much more balanced, not wanting to tear up the older man.

"I don't think he'll say anything anymore; Tim is dead," Bernardt said, not wanting to elaborate on the circumstances.

"Oh, poor soul..." Noir said sadly.

The mysterious outline of the teleportation device was visible on the hill, and in the valley, the pleasantly blowing wind turned into a gale, whipping the half-torn "Open" sign that still hung there, swaying.